WHEN OUR JACK WENT TO WAR

—

WHEN OUR JACK WENT TO WAR

—

(A fictional story based on a real-life event)

SANDY McKAY

Longacre

The assistance of Creative New Zealand is gratefully
acknowledged by the author and publisher.

A LONGACRE BOOK published by Random House New Zealand
18 Poland Road, Glenfield, Auckland, New Zealand

For more information about our titles go to www.randomhouse.co.nz

A catalogue record for this book is available from
the National Library of New Zealand

Random House New Zealand is part of the Random House Group
New York   London   Sydney   Auckland   Delhi   Johannesburg

First published 2013

ISBN 978 1 77553 309 2
eISBN 978 1 77553 310 8

Design: Megan van Staden
Cover image: Clayton Bastiani/Trevillion Images
All newspaper clippings sourced from the National Library of
New Zealand Papers Past website (paperspast.natlib.govt.nz)

Printed in New Zealand by Printlink

This publication is printed on paper pulp sourced from sustainably
grown and managed forests, using Elemental Chlorine Free (ECF)
bleaching, and printed with 100% vegetable-based inks.

This title is also available as an eBook

THE GREAT WAR

BRITAIN AND GERMANY

ON THE BELGIAN FRONTIER

BELGIANS PUTTING UP A BIG FIGHT

BOMBARDMENT OF BELGRADE

ENTHUSIASM CONTINUES IN ENGLAND

SWISS PREPARED TO DEFEND THEIR NEUTRALITY

BRITAIN DECLARES WAR

1916

OCTOBER

When our Jack went to war our mother cried and cried. Poor Ma — she really didn't want him to go. But it was 1916 and the war in Europe had been under way for nearly three years. It was called 'the war to end all wars' and it was going to be over by Christmas, which is why they needed all the fit young men they could get — to help force the Germans to surrender.

Loads of Jack's friends were going off to fight. Some had already left. Tom Baxter from Blacks Road joined up last year. So did Walter McSkimming from Outram.

Ma wasn't happy about our Jack going though.

'It'll be fine, Ma,' said Jack, trying to talk her round. 'I'll be home before you know it. You'll see.'

'It just doesn't seem right,' said Ma. 'Going off to the other side of the world to fight a war that's got nothing to do with us.'

'But it has, Ma,' said Jack. 'England's war is OUR war. That's what the Prime Minister says.'

Jack grinned. Then he put on his silly deep voice and narrowed his eyes like our Dad used to do, right before he gave us a ticking off.

'Remember, loyal countrymen — it is your DUTY to fight for king and country.' Jack pointed his finger straight at Ma. 'And you must do whatever is in your power to resist our common enemy. And help defend the mother country.'

Ma still wasn't convinced. But these days there wasn't much choice. If your name was in the ballot you had no option but to sign up.

Ma shook her head, sipped her tea and gazed out the window.

'What is our world coming to?' she said.

Since our Dad died Ma could gaze out the kitchen window for hours on end, wondering what our world was coming to. Sometimes she gazed for so long she forgot to put the dinner on.

The window faced the patch of manuka scrub where Dad used to chop firewood. His old axe was still jammed into a tree stump next to the lavvy but Ma wouldn't let anyone take it out.

'It was the last thing your father did before he died,' she would say, with a tear in her eye.

When I first saw our Jack in his uniform I wished it was me. I'd never seen my brother so spruced up before. His jacket had buttons and pockets all over the place. And around his middle was a big brown belt. His boots were well shined up and the hat looked top notch. I'd never seen Jack in a hat before.

Blimey. He looked so grown up — and important and brave. There was only one thing missing.

'Where's ya gun, Jack?' I said.

'He'll have it soon enough,' muttered Ma.

'Is it a .22 like our Dad's?'

Jack laughed. 'No. It's not a .22, Tom. I think it's Germans we're supposed to be shooting, not rabbits.'

Jack loved Dad's .22. He could shoot a rabbit from 150 yards away. I couldn't wait to have a go but I wasn't allowed to use it.

I wanted to be in the army too, but I hadn't turned thirteen yet. You were supposed to be eighteen years old to enlist but Frank Morrison's brother said you could get in at sixteen if you passed the fitness test.

Still . . . even though I was fit as a fiddle and nearly as tall as Jack already, I would never pass for eighteen. And besides, if *I* went off to war who'd be left to help at home? It'd be all up to Ma and she had enough to do with looking after the garden and the fowls and everything. Not to mention our Amy who hadn't started school yet.

It was hard not having our Dad around. He died not long after the war started. Poor Ma. She cried and cried. I did too. But I didn't cry quite as much as Ma.

Thank heavens for Mrs Jenkins. That's when she started coming over regularly — 'just to keep an eye on everyone'.

Mrs Jenkins lived around the corner, in Frame Street. Her first name was Nola but only Ma was allowed to call her that. They'd been friends for a long time, Ma and Mrs J. And she was on the back doorstep the moment she heard about our Jack signing up. They must have sat in the kitchen for ages talking because when I got up to go to the lavvy the two of them were still there — huddled by the coal range and warming their hands over another mug of tea.

I couldn't hear what they were saying exactly, but I knew it was serious and I knew it was about the war. I could tell by the way Mrs J whispered and stirred her teaspoon round and round and round.

It all happened pretty fast and once our Jack was signed up he was on his way to Trentham Camp quicker than you could say 'Jack Robinson'.

The whole family went to the railway station to wave him goodbye. Ma wore her best hat, the one with the red feather. And Amy wore her brown pinafore. I wore Jack's old best trousers and my new best shirt.

'Make sure you write to me every day,' I yelled to Jack.

'I'll do my best,' he said, with a grin.

'That's our Jack alright,' said Mrs J, rubbing lipstick from our Jack's cheek with her hanky.

Our Jack always did his best. He was a beaut runner and a dab hand with a pencil too. One of his drawings of Brighton Beach got hung up in the church hall last year. Everyone admired it. Mrs J said it was good enough to pass for a photograph. 'I'd be proud to have it on my mantel any day,' she said.

Our Jack was clever alright. There was nothing he couldn't turn his hand to. After he left school he did odd jobs on farms around the place. Then, early last year, he started training to be a carpenter. He got an apprenticeship with Mr Kidd from North East Valley Joinery. Mr Kidd gave Jack his own personal nail bag — with a buckle that tied round your waist and initials carved inside the strap. But Ma said Jack's building career would have to wait till he got back from the war.

We kept Jack's letters in a biscuit tin on the shelf in the kitchen, right next to the hook for his nail bag. The tin had pink roses on it — and a lid that didn't close properly after it got stood on accidentally by our Dad. Some of the letters were addressed to Ma and Amy and some were just addressed to me. The letters were often held back by the authorities, for security reasons. And sometimes they'd arrive three or four at a time. It was up to me to sort them out. To put them in the right order. I liked doing that, sprawling them out on the mat to see which one came first. We read them together on Friday nights when Mrs J came over to play cards.

Our Jack's first letter came all the way from Trentham army camp. I took the stamp off the envelope straight away and soaked it in a saucer of water — all ready for my album. I'd collected eleven stamps so far. Most of them looked the same. They were nearly all of King George, but in different colours.

With our Jack going overseas I thought I might start collecting coins as well.

JACK'S FIRST LETTER

1916

OCTOBER

October 1916

Dear Tom,

Well, mate. Looks like I finally got here, safe and sound.

Your big brother is in the army for real now. Private Jack Donald William McAllister — 275530, 2nd Battalion, Otago Regiment, NZEF. (That stands for New Zealand Expeditionary Force.)

We clattered into Trentham last Wednesday arvo on the train. There're a few of us from down home. Some of them you know — like Tom Hendry and Ted Macleod. Cyril Jackson's here too. And Stuart Croft. And Billy Prescott. Billy Prescott is in the same section as me.

The place is a bit different than I expected. It's been grey and drizzly since we arrived so everything's pretty well soaked through. There are eight in our tent, all packed in like sardines. Billy Prescott and I are together — Stuart Croft is in the next row over.

Things have been slow to get cranked up due to the crook weather and we've been confined to barracks for days. I spent all of yesterday arvo sewing on buttons so I'm getting a dab hand at threading a needle, if nothing else. Only stabbed myself twice — so not too much of a bloodbath yet.

Best regards,
Jack

I read the letter out loud to Ma and Amy and Mrs J who sat round the kitchen table, peeling potatoes for dinner.

'Let's hope that's all the blood he gets to see,' said Mrs J, cutting a knobbly bit off with her knife.

'Blood? What blood?' said Ma, in a panic.

Mrs J laughed. 'From the sewing needle, Jess.'

'Oh, yes. Of course,' said Ma. Then they both took another slurp of tea and went quiet. They always went quiet when the subject of the war came up. Mrs J's lips would go all thin with pursing and her cheeks dented inwards, like she was sucking the life out of them. And Ma would get her 'what's the world coming to?' stare on again.

Ma and Mrs J weren't too keen on the war. Not like Mr Gilbertson. He was the butcher on the corner of Felix Street and North Road. He wore a black and white striped apron and always gave us kids free saveloys. Mr Gilbertson loved to talk about the war.

It was Allies this and Allies that. Germans this and Germans that. He liked to jabber on about the Russians and the French and the Yankees. And other wars too. Wars with funny names. Like Boer and Crimea. Mr Gilbertson reckoned if he was a few years younger he'd be signing up quicker than you could say 'Jack Robinson'.

'Give those bolshy Huns a good seeing to,' he said.

Jack's next letter came three days later.

Trentham Camp

Dear Tom,

I'm pleased to report that the rain has finally stopped and yesterday we had our first route march. Blimey! I didn't know a chap could walk so far. Nine miles, in one day! Talk about tuckered out. You don't get much chance of a sit down at the finish either — not without a bollocking from the Sergeant.

'Did you think you joined the army for a bloody holiday, McAllister?'

Our Sarge has a voice like a foghorn and it's a wonder you didn't hear him all the way across the Cook Strait. I wouldn't mess with him though. He's built like a brick lavvy and I know who'd come off second best.

Route marches are hard work, Tom. And the Sarge makes it just about as hard as he can. You have to march with all your gear on, which means a full uniform as well as your pack. Last night my back ached like billy-o and today I can barely stand up.

I can't imagine going into battle with a load like that! The pack weighs a jolly ton and some of the smaller lads are struggling. Billy reckons he hasn't worked so hard in his life.

I'm no slouch when it comes to fitness and I'm

no stranger to hard yakka either. But it's different work to what I'm used to.

Some of the 'townies' are doing it hard. There's one chap, Arnold Wilson, who came straight from the Mornington Post Office. I don't think he's done anything more physical than lick a stamp since he left school.

Don't get me wrong. Arnold's a nice chap and I'm sure he has a fine knowledge of postage stamps but I think he might be a bit soft for a soldier. Cyril Jackson nicknamed him Stampy and it looks like it's going to stick. I s'pose there are worse names to be stuck with, eh.

Anyway, I can't see old Stampy shooting too many Germans. But I guess no one knows until we get there.

Best regards,
Jack

Jack's letters were chocka-full of army stuff. He wrote about route marches and drills and what the food was like. Trentham was a different world alright but it sounded a sight more interesting than North East Valley.

I always wrote back as soon as I could. Ma let me use her fountain pen sometimes. But mostly I used a pencil. I kept it sharp with Dad's old pocket knife and if there was no paper I wrote on the back of an old envelope.

Usually I did a pencil sketch as well. And sometimes I let Amy do a scribble, but only if she stayed in the lines. I wanted it neat and tidy. These letters were going all the way to Wellington and you never knew who might be seeing them. Jack sometimes drew on the back of his envelope as well.

There was a lot to talk about. And I wanted to know every last detail.

COURT-MARTIAL.

PECULIAR EVIDENCE TENDERED

PALMERSTON NORTH, Nov. 15.

At the court-martial of Michael Kellalea, peculiar evidence was disclosed.

Accused said he had lived in a dugout and subsequently in a cave in the back district of Waitotara for several months. He was afraid to come out, because his employer terrorised him by the statement that if he came out he would be shot.

Accused's employer, it was alleged, did sentry-go while accused cut bush for him.

Sentence was deferred.

Other action will probably follow.

Dear Jack,

Poor old Stampy, eh. What do you think's going to happen when he meets his first German? Let's hope he doesn't lose his nerve and scarper. Marian Murdoch says you can get shot for that. Or sentenced to hard labour at least. She had a cousin up north whose friend was court-martialled. There was a piece in the paper about it.

Do you know how much longer you will have to stay in Trentham Camp for? I bet you're dying to get off overseas. Will you have to go to England first? Marian's brother's in France just now. I don't know how big France is but it looks quite small on the map. You might run into him if you get there. She's always going on about him. Marian reckons he's shot heaps of Germans already.

Pow! Pow! Lucky you!

I wish I could join the army, Jack. It's boring here at home with Ma moping about and no one half-decent to yarn with. Amy starts school soon so I've been helping her write her name. We found an old slate in the shed.

The best thing about Amy's name is that it's only got three letters. I reckon school's hard enough without having a long name to write.

Talking of names . . . now that I'm acting 'man of the house' I've been trying to come up with a suitably serious signature. These are my efforts so far. Which one do you like best? The one with the curly A or the one with the curly M? I think I'm leaning towards the curly A.

Lots of love from your brother,

Thomas Andrew McAllister

Dear Tom,

The curly A looks classy, mate. Top notch, I'd say.

I did hear about Marian's brother getting wounded and he was lucky not to be killed by the sound of it. Must be tough at times and there've been plenty of lucky escapes. Some serious fighting in France by all accounts but I think we've given them a run for their money. Here at Trentham Camp the war still seems a long way off. Most of our days are filled with routine drills and marching, which is starting to wear pretty hard on the feet. At this rate they'll be worn out before we get there. You should see my blisters, Tom. The leather boots are stiff as corpses and twice as rough.

The march on Saturday went forever and a couple of chaps dropped out along the way. Old Stampy had to have a sit-down in the middle. I'd hate to see him tackle a march like that in scorching heat.

Sergeant Harvey didn't bother hiding his opinion of the lads who weren't up to the task.

Our Sarge has a reputation as a bit of a tyrant. Nothing escapes his beady watch. Billy Prescott reckons he goes to bed in his khakis and sleeps with his eyes open. Ha! I wouldn't put it past him.

Speaking of sleep, I really must try and get some. Got to keep up my strength for tomorrow.

Love to everyone at home.

Best regards,

Jack

Dear Jack,

Marching round hills sounds way more exciting than doing sums. I reckon I could even put up with blisters, if I had to. Better than doing arithmetic by a long shot.

The worst thing is the times tables. The twos and fives are okay but I don't do so well with the sevens. Beats me how you're supposed to remember what six times seven equals. Or seven times four.

And Mrs Stains cracks me over the knuckles with her ruler when I get one wrong. I think she expects me to be as clever as you, Jack. But I don't see how cracking someone over the knuckles is going to help. In fact, I reckon it only makes it worse.

Oh well . . . At least I haven't had the strap in a while. Malcolm Davis got the strap last Friday because he couldn't do his takeaways. And Mrs Stains said if he can't do takeaways at his age then heaven help him. Malcolm didn't like her saying that and said, 'Well, why doesn't heaven help me, then?' Ten minutes later he was sitting outside the headmaster's office as punishment for being cheeky.

Blimey, Jack! I don't think I'll ever get these tables learned. I'm okay saying them out loud but, when it comes to a test, they go clean out of my head. I can't wait to leave school and not have sums to do. Mind you, Ma says if I want to be a carpenter like you I'll have to be knowing how to measure properly.

I might try and get Uncle Ced to help. He's coming over in the weekend. And he promised to take me rabbit shooting. I don't have Ma's permission yet but Uncle Ced reckons he can talk her round. He says he was only eleven years old when he shot his first bunny and Ma must have a short memory if she thinks otherwise.

I'm not holding my breath for Ma's permission though.

To tell the truth she's gone a bit cranky since you left, Jack. She won't let me out of her sight for five minutes. So it's good to have Uncle Ced on my side. Uncle Ced's a cracker. Last time he came round he told Ma I was the man of the house now and that means I should be knowing how to hunt.

He said if our Jack can go overseas and kill Germans then surely I can stay home and kill rabbits. Ma went a bit quiet after that.

Lots of love

From Tom

PS — I hope you like the fruit cake. We made it last weekend. And we used up a whole cup of sultanas, which meant no rice pudding for Sunday. So tuck in and enjoy. And remember, it's not just soldiers making an effort for the war these days.

Trentham Camp

Dear Tom,

Thanks a heap for the tucker, mate. I am ashamed to report that your delicious cake came to a rather sorry end after I hid it under my stretcher. When I got back from the route march, a rat had beaten me to it! He'd toothed it over good and proper.

I know, Tom — it was my own jolly fault and serves me right. Still . . . I'd be grateful if you could send more and next time I promise to share it with the lads.

I might have a touch of homesickness. And I think I may be missing Ma's cooking more than I thought. The food here is not worth writing home about so I won't bother.

It's a strange old feeling being stuck in Trentham. A bit like no-man's-land, I expect. Still no word about when we set sail though. Oh, well . . .

Cheerio and take care,

Best regards to everyone,

Jack McAllister (Private)

Dear Jack McAllister (Private),

I promise I'll make you another cake, just as soon as we can lay our hands on more sultanas.

Good news! Uncle Ced came round on Sunday and Ma let me go hunting.

Our uncle has the gift of the gab, as you know, and we must have caught Ma in a weak moment. He reckons it was the thought of rabbit stew that sealed the deal. I reckon so too. Ma said she hadn't had a good rabbit stew since our Dad was alive. Then Uncle Ced gave me a wink and said he might be knowing how to fix that.

So off we went, all the way along Lindsay Creek and up Mount Cargill Road. And guess what! I'd shot two rabbits by lunchtime. One of them was more than fifty yards away. Uncle Ced reckons I must have a good eye for hunting.

We came home with six dead bunnies altogether. It was great! The best part was at the end when Uncle Ced took the skins off with his special knife and we hung them on the back fence to dry. Talk about blood and guts, Jack! It was cracker!

Lots of love

From Tom

PS — I hope you like my sketch. That's me in the tussock grass and that's Uncle Ced beside me. In case you didn't notice, he's the one in the hat. I'm the one with the skinny legs and the gun. And see that little smear of blood in the right-hand corner? That's fair dinkum bunny blood.

Trentham Camp

Dear Tom,

Well done on the rabbit front, eh. I can see I'll be in for some serious competition when I get home. I hope Ma rose to the occasion and made a nice hearty stew for you all.

Speaking of which, I could really go one of Ma's hotpots right now. Complete with all the trimmings . . . Thick juicy gravy, creamy mashed spuds and plenty of carrots, onion and swede. The mouth's fair watering at the thought. No such luxury here, I'm afraid. Just more sloppy dishwater soup. Yesterday it was potato and leek, only I'm yet to see any trace of leek!

No point in complaining though. Sergeant Harvey says we should have our minds on more important things. Like marching together in strict military formation, for example!

Things are getting serious now. Yesterday we were shown how to use a hand grenade and I'd have to say pulling the pin isn't as easy as it looks. The Sarge says it's all in the arm action and it took me a good while to get the hang of it. I have a feeling I'm going to need more practice before they let me loose on the Hun, put it that way.

It started me thinking though. What's it going to be like with a real grenade, eh? I mean, it's all very well practising but what's going to happen when your target is a fair dinkum person? The thought of it scares the jeepers out of me.

Oh well, the Sarge reckons, when it comes to the crunch, we won't give killing enemy soldiers a second thought.

Let's hope he's right.

Best regards,

Jack

PS — I've been thinking about Erik Hoffman at school. His father came from Germany and, apart from eating a swag of red cabbage, there was no way you could tell. So, what if the enemy soldiers look just like him?

How's that going to feel?

Just a thought.

DISLOYAL UTTERANCE

INDISCRETION IN RAILWAY CARRIAGE.

Another example of stupid indiscretion was furnished in the Magistrate's Court to-day, when George Adam Hesse was called upon to answer the following charge:—That on or about 25th or 26th January, in a railway carriage between Waiouru and Wellington did make use of the following language calculated to interfere with recruiting:—"A man is a ——— fool for going to the front. I am a ——— German and you have never gained an inch on them yet. You are a lot of ——— fools to fight."

When asked to plead the accused said: "I plead guilty as far as the language is concerned, but I did not mean it to be taken seriously."

The Magistrate (Mr. W. G. Riddell, S.M.):—"Well you should keep your mouth shut if you don't want to be taken seriously."

Accused proceeded to further explain his conduct, but was abruptly cut short by the Magistrate. "You are fined £3, in default 14 days," was his Worship's decision.

Dear Jack,

I didn't know Erik Hoffman came from Germany. Fancy that. People who came here from Germany are getting a hard time of it these days. The neighbours are starting to look at them sideways. Like they've suddenly grown two heads or something. It doesn't seem fair 'cause they were okay before, weren't they.

Why can't we fight someone else?

Frank Morrison's grandad can't work out why we're fighting the Germans in the first place. He said it's usually the French you have to watch. Them and the Russians. He said in the last war Germany was on our side.

Not this time though.

Mrs Stains gave us a history lesson last week. She said the reason the New Zealanders have to fight in the war is because Germany invaded Belgium and Britain made a promise to help Belgium. We have to help Britain because we're part of the Empire and when Britain declared war, so did we. She made a diagram on the board.

It all sounded very complicated when Mrs Stains tried to explain and Frank started flicking bits of wood around with his ruler. He ended up copping 'six of the best' from the headmaster. So I didn't get to hear the reason why we're friends with the French again. I suppose it'll work itself out in the end.

Anyway, I've saved the best news for last. You'll never guess. Not in a million years!

Last week we got a dog. Yep. Fair dinkum. I know Ma always said we couldn't have one, but in the end she couldn't say no. Mrs J's terrier had pups and she brought one over. I wish you could see him, Jack. He's black and tan in the body and his paws are real fluffy and big as paddles, which means he's going to grow into a very large animal. But he fits into the palm of your hand just now and his ears are soft as velvet.

Lots of love,
Tom

OAMARU, This Day.

William Henry Derrick, charged with publishing seditious utterances—"Colonials are, damned rotters. Three cheers for Germany"—pleaded guilty, and was sentenced to 22 months' imprisonment in Dunedin Gaol. The Magistrate said the remarks were an added insult, as they were made to a woman who had lost her son at the front recently.

Dear Tom,

A new pup, mate? Crikey! Things are looking up. Make sure you train him properly. Let him know who's in charge right from the start and don't stand for any nonsense. If you don't let him away with too much he'll turn out good as gold. Start as you mean to go on, eh. About time you had some responsibility. It'll do you the world of good.

I don't have much time to write today. Too busy polishing boots and darning socks.

Take care little brother.

Best regards,

Jack

Dear Jack,

What a week we've had. Last Wednesday was our Dad's birthday. Did you remember?

Poor Ma. She didn't take it too good. In fact she didn't get out of bed till lunchtime. And that was only after Mrs J came over. Mrs J doesn't like people not getting out of bed and she flung the curtains nearly off their tracks in protest.

After that it was all hands on deck. First she made Amy and me have a bath. Then she made me chop the wood and get the coal range going 'cause it had gone out two days ago. Amy had to get her hair washed because Mrs J thought it was ripe for nits and 'we better get onto it' before the nit nurse came and dunked her head in kerosene. Talk about bossy.

She even gave our new dog a seeing to with the scrubbing brush. He didn't know what hit him.

By the time Mrs J left, things were up and running like clockwork. And probably just as well. Amy and me don't know what to do when Ma gets that stare on. She either sits by the window in a daze or takes to her bed. Mrs J says it's called grief and Ma has a bad dose of it. When I asked how long it was going to last, she said there was no way of telling, but it might go for another twelve months and it was up to us to pitch in and make things easier.

Twelve months! Jeepers! Can you imagine Ma moping around for that long? It doesn't seem fair. I miss our Dad too, of course I do. But crying all day doesn't do any good. Like Mrs J said, better to keep busy.

Amy made a card for Dad's birthday and we took it down to the cemetery. She drew a picture of our new dog on the front and we took a jar of sweet peas. The sweet peas came from down the back of the fowl house. We took jam sandwiches too. There was just Amy, me and Mrs J. Ma stayed at home with a headache. But she promised she'd come next time.

Hope all is good with you, Jack.

Lots of love,

Tom

Dear Tom,

Joves, mate. I'd forgotten all about our Dad's birthday. The day and dates mean nothing up here. Do you know how old he would have been? I reckon he would have been coming up fifty. Poor Ma. I hope she's feeling better now.

Things are a bit hectic here. We're all recovering from a visit by our Governor General so there hasn't been much time to think. What a palaver, eh. The Governor General came to thank all the 'fine colonial men' for serving Mother England. It was all very formal with plenty of saluting.

To be honest, I don't think the lads were taken in by the 'Mother England' talk. It's not like we're professional soldiers or anything. At the end of the day we're just a bunch of lads keen to see some action.

I think Billy Prescott spoke for us all when he said, 'We don't mind giving a hand, Sir, but we need to get there before it's over. And we need to stop practising and get on with the real thing.'

He's right about that. None of us joined the army to be stuck in Trenthan sewing on buttons and the sooner we get on with the job, the better.

Best regards,

Jack

Dear Jack,

Hey! Guess what? We've finally come up with a name for
our dog. *Jacky*. It was Amy's idea and Mrs J thinks it's a
cracker. So now you've got a brand new dog named after
you. And I'd have to say he really suits it. Amy says he's
got your nose and he's certainly got your big paddle feet!

Must go now and feed the fowls.

Love from

Tom

Trentham Camp

Dear Tom,

My big paddle feet are taking a real hammering from all this endless marching.

We had bayonet practice yesterday arvo. What a lark. There were kit bags flung over a cross bar, just like a soccer goal. And when the Sarge yelled 'Advance', we all marched towards the bag, plunging bayonets in as we went. 'In . . . Out . . . In . . . Out . . . In . . . Out . . .' bellowed the Sarge. 'Harder. Faster. Come on boys! Give it a twist!'

It was quite comical really and some of the lads were in stitches. But the Sarge doesn't like to see a soldier enjoying himself and afterwards he gave us all a proper talking to. He said it was about time we took our training seriously. Then he rabbited on about what an important task lay ahead.

'You must never forget what you're fighting for,' he said, sternly.

'And what's that again, Sir?' said Billy.

The next bit was laugh-out-loud funny. Because the Sarge got this real serious expression on his face and said, 'Freedom. Humanity. And Civilisation!'

Blimey, Tom! He did it with such a straight face that it was hard not to crack up. We knew we'd be in for a big lot of press-ups if we did, though.

Like I said, the army can be an odd place at

times. And anyone joining up would be well advised to pack his sense of humour.

Please pass on my regards to Mrs J. And tell her I am grateful she is taking such good care of our Ma.

Best regards,

Your brother,

Jack

Dear Jack,

Bayonets, eh. After I read your last letter Frank Morrison and me had a go ourselves. We stuffed pea straw from the strawberry patch into pillowcases and had a 'stab-up' in the shed. It was all good fun until Ma cottoned on and starting going crook about the state of her kitchen knife. I guess she had a point because there was no doubt about it — her best knife had certainly lost its cutting edge.

Jeepers! It won't cut much of anything now and Ma can't use the steel to make it sharp again, which means we're going to have to ask Uncle Ced next time he visits. Ma hates asking Uncle Ced for help. She says he's got his own family to look after and we shouldn't be worrying him with our troubles.

But that's a load of rot because Uncle Ced doesn't mind in the least. He's feeling bad about not being able to join up and likes to make himself useful. Well, that's what he told me.

Did you know Uncle Ced tried to get in the army, Jack? Turns out he was too old by just thirteen months. I don't see what difference thirteen months would make. I thought they needed all the soldiers they can get. But schoolteachers don't have to go and some of the farmers don't either. It said so in the paper. There were people writing letters to complain.

There must be loads of people in the army now, Jack. I know heaps of kids at school whose brothers and uncles have signed up. Some are only sixteen or seventeen. Sally Johnston's brother is at Trentham like you. And Eddie's oldest brother is in France. Lily Brinsdon's uncle is in a hospital in England after copping a bullet in the shoulder.

Some have come back already. Like Marian Murdoch's brother, for example. He got half his leg blown off by a German shell. Marian said he might have to stay in a wheelchair for a very long time. Maybe even the rest of his life.

This war is affecting everything, Jack. At school last week there was a massive fight in the playground. And Peter Hammer got thumped by Bert Thompson for no reason. Bert Thompson just went for Peter, grabbed him by the collar and gave him a right seeing to. The next day Peter Hammer's eye was so swollen he couldn't see the blackboard. So they both got sent to the headmaster's office straight away. No one knew what started it, but Colin Griffiths reckons it was all over Peter Hammer's uncle being a 'conchie'. We didn't know exactly what a conchie was. Darrol Fibbs thought it was some kind of chestnut. But then Frank Morrison looked it up in the dictionary and we could only find the word 'conch' which means shellfish.

Must go now, Jack.

Best regards,

Tom

DRAWING OF FIRST BALLOT.

WELLINGTON, October 29.

The first ballot of members of the Second Division of the New Zealand Expeditionary Force Reserve was commenced by the Government Statistician (Mr Malcolm Fraser) at 9 o'clock this morning, when he started to draw on Class A. (married men without children). The supervising Magistrate is Mr S. E. McCarthy, and Mr J. P. Luke, Mayor of Wellington, is in attendance.

The total number of men in Class A. is 15,292, and of these 5000 are being drawn.

The ballot, it is expected, will be completed by to-morrow morning, and the result will be announced by Government "Gazette" on Tuesday of next week.

In addition, 1500 men, being accretions from the First Division (men coming of age, etc.) will be called up on the same occasion without the taking of a ballot. The "Gazette" next week will thus contain 6500 names, being 1500 accretions from the First Division, and 5000 married men without children.

There will then be 10,292 men still left in Class A, Second Division, which it is estimated will prove sufficient for another two drafts. The men now being drawn will not be required to mobilise before March next.

Trentham Camp

Dear Tom,

'Conchie' is short for 'conscientious objector', which is someone who refuses to be conscripted. It's not a popular call to make these days for obvious reasons. They've got some conchies locked up in huts here in Trentham Camp. They have to stay here till they get shipped out and, believe me, the conditions are even worse than prison.

Yesterday, me and Stuart Croft were put in charge of a group of them. The poor beggars aren't allowed to go anywhere and have to be guarded twenty-four hours a day. The guards work in shifts — four hours on and four hours off. Don't get me wrong, I don't have much sympathy for the conchies, but I know they don't have an easy time of it either.

Best regards,
Jack

A QUAKER SENTENCED.

(FROM OUR OWN CORRESPONDENT.)

LONDON, 24th August.

For refusing to handle a rifle at Whitley Bay, Northumberland, Mr. John P. F. Fletcher, a Quaker, has been sentenced to two years' hard labour. Mr. Fletcher is a well-known pacifist in this country as well as in Australasia, and it is recalled that he was organiser of the Australian Freedom League, 1912-1913, and president of the Christchurch (New Zealand) Anti-Militarist League for 1913, and served two terms of imprisonment in New Zealand during that year for anti-conscription propaganda. He also served a sentence of two months in Pentonville in 1916, as one of the five members of the executive of the No-Conscription Fellowship, who went to prison for publishing a pamphlet entitled "Repeal the Act."

THE FINGER OF SCORN.

Speaking at Grimsby after the presentation of medals to soldiers of the Manchester and Lincoln Regiments for gallant conduct in the field and for service at home, Major-General Sir Stanley Von Donop made some pointed remarks about men who refused military duty and service to the King and country. "You have such men in your midst," he said, "and we have to administer military law and treat them as soldiers. I know some of you think these men are leniently dealt with when they are merely sent to prison whilst you have to go out and fight. But you must remember that they will be haunted for the rest of their lives. They refused duty when it called. They will have the finger of scorn pointed at them, whilst you will have the praise."

Dear Jack,

The people round here don't have any time for conchies
either. Peter Hammer doesn't go to our school any more,
not after the fight. And Richard McGregor's Ma said his
family was going to move away because of it. They have to
go down south to look for work because no one will give
them any here.

I think that's daft.

But when I said so to Ma she said, 'Well, I don't see
why our Jack should have to fight if the others don't.
Why should they be allowed to stay home safe and sound
while Jack does all the dirty work?'

She was starting to get cranky again so I decided to
keep the rest of my thoughts to myself.

Love from

Tom

REFUSING TO PARADE.

Auckland, November 16.

Harold Wright was found guilty by court-martial to-day of refusing to parade for medical examination when ordered to do so. The officer commanding the Group gave evidence that he gave the order personally, the accused saying in a courteous and straightforward manner that he would not attend.

The accused stated that he was a member of the Society of Friends, and objected to service.

Trentham Camp

Dear Tom,

It's true about the war changing things and your observations are spot on. The whole of Europe's getting a royal shake-up and no one knows how it's going to turn out. I guess we can only try to get through as best we can and not dwell on things too much.

So how's your Jacky getting on these days, eh? Have you got a kennel sorted yet? I think there's some corrugated iron down by the fowl house that might do the job. I was going to use it for a new shed but that can wait till I get back. There might even be some nails in an old honey tin under Dad's workbench. If you run short, don't be shy about using my nail bag. It's hanging on a hook in the kitchen. I'm sure Uncle Ced would give you a hand if you asked him.

There are a few things you'll have to consider before you start building. Like you'll need to make sure the pitch of the roof is high enough for the rain to run off. And a bit of spouting wouldn't go astray either. I'm sure you'll figure it out, Tom. Just take your time and watch your measuring.

How's everything else going? Are you managing to feed the fowls okay? And how are those spuds down the side of the house? They'll need to be shoaled up pretty soon, if I remember rightly. If they were planted in time you might get a nice wee feed for Christmas.

Things are looking up here weather-wise. The rain has eased off this week and the days are getting warmer. The lads are making the most of the more settled weather.

Billy Prestcott, Cyril Jackson, Arnold Wilson and I scored some leave in the weekend. We went to a hotel in Wellington for the night. It was great to see our capital city for the first time. A bit like Dunedin, I thought.

On Saturday we had a stroll round parliament buildings before going for a look at the zoo. You'd love the animals there, Tom, especially the elephants. We took the tram. I was thinking that when this war is over, we could all visit the zoo together. You, me, Ma and Amy. Mrs J could come too if she wanted. And Uncle Ced. It'd be great.

We could catch the ferry to Wellington and stay a few days. That'd be plenty long enough to have a look around and it'd be something fun to look forward to.

There is an elephant that you can ride for a penny. I have a lot of respect for elephants. Did you know they are completely vegetarian? It's hard to imagine something of that size living entirely on vegetables. And they must have to eat a lot to maintain their body weight. By Joves, they must.

Three of us had a ride on one. And when we climbed back down the zoo-keeper spun us a yarn about elephants being good luck. He gave us a postcard each, too. I've put mine in my wallet for safe keeping.

   Love from
   Jack

PS — I hope you like my elephant sketch.

PPS — Does Ma have any plans for Christmas Day, yet?

Dear Jack,

I think Ma has been trying not to think too much about Christmas Day. But she does think the zoo is a great idea. So do I.

Ma says we can book the tickets just as soon as you get back home. She was quite perked up after reading that and made a batch of girdle scones to celebrate. We ate them hot with Mrs J's gooseberry jam. Better than bread and dripping sandwiches any day.

I'd really love to see a live elephant. Frank's dad rode on one last year. He's got a photograph to prove it. I had a go at drawing one but it wasn't my best effort.

Yesterday Mrs Stains helped me look up elephants in the encyclopaedia. It turns out the Indian ones have smaller ears than the African ones. I managed to trace one in my sketchbook before I had to put the encyclopaedia back.

Things are different at school this term. We have new routines — like saying the Lord's Prayer at morning assembly, for example. And sometimes we have to say the 23rd Psalm as well. That's the one about the shepherd not wanting to lie down in pastures. If you get the words wrong you have to stay in after school and practise.

Luckily I know all the words off by heart on account of Sunday school.

You are so lucky to have finally escaped Sunday school, Jack. I don't think I'll ever get away from it. Frank Morrison doesn't have to go after he turns thirteen. Neither does Richard McGregor.

Not me though. Ma says I should stay and help with the young ones. Blimey! Since our Dad's accident she's got even stricter than ever.

It took a lot of persuading to let me go to the pictures last week. It was a Charlie Chaplin movie called *Laughing Gas*. Me and Frank snuck in the back stalls. Charlie Chaplin makes me laugh out loud. I don't like his moustache much but his hat's top notch.

They had news reels at the pictures too. And music. I wonder what sort of music they have in Germany. Probably just a load of old war marches, eh. What do you think?

Frank thought one of the soldiers on the news reel looked a bit like you, Jack. And after I agreed, he said, 'What do you reckon your Jack's doing this very minute?' We were having a few guesses when a lady behind us whacked Frank square in the back with her handbag and told us both to keep our voices down and watch the film. I think people round here are losing their sense of humour. And Mrs J says nothing's going to change till the war ends.

Speaking of the war ending, have you heard about the new weapon they've got? It's called a tank. It's got wheels like a tractor and they think it's going to help us win the war. They say the Germans won't know what's hit them.

Any news about when you're off to England yet?

Lots of love,

From Tom

"What Happened at 22" is a melo-
drama in which the stream of incidents
never rests until the last breathless
scene.   The plot is everlastingly pre-
senting surprises, and through the clever
wiles of a pretty secretary a dangerous
forger and murderer is brought to book.
The supporting pictures include "A
Merry Mix-up" (comedy),   the latest
Pathe Gazette, and Charlie Chaplin in
"Laughing Gas."

CHRISTMAS IN CAMP

A Trentham Treat

The Plum-Pudding Parade

FOR THE MEN IN CAMP.

Though general leave is to be granted the men in camp at Christmas, it is known that there will still be a large number of men who elect for one reason or another to remain in camp. There are some hundreds of them, for instance, who have no home to go to in New Zealand, or whose homes are too distant for them to undertake the journey in the time at their disposal. Or it may be that some have just left their own districts and do not care to return so soon, not even to partake of the joys of Christmas among their own people. Whoever they be, the Mayoress (Mrs. Luke) and the ladies of her very hard-working committee intend to see that they are not going to suffer by sticking to the camp, and to that end extensive preparations are now being made by the ladies mentioned with encouraging results.

In the Christmas bounty to be disbursed absolutely no differentiation will be made. The soldier from Hokianga will be as welcome as the one who hails from Wellington Terrace, and he who comes from Half-Moon Bay will have the same status at the feast as the "gentleman in khaki" from Heretaunga. It will be an all-in-day, as it was last year, and those who remember the joyous banquet that marked last Christmas Day at Trentham and at Maymorn will bear its impress on their memories to their dying day.

Mrs. Luke will once more lead the attack, but she naturally wants all the help she can get to brighten the camp festival on Christmas Day. So far she has received promises as follow:—Gear Meat Company, 25 lambs and 100lb. of suet (for the puddings); Nelson Bros., 20 lambs; E. Barber and Co., 15 lambs; N.Z. Refrigerating Company, Wanganui, same as other meat companies; Wellington Meat Preserving Co. will boil the puddings; Mayoress's Countess of Liverpool Fund, £200; Dunedin Fund, £100; Auckland, Canterbury, and Southland promises help; Marlborough Patriotic Society, £15. Contributions are also to be made by the Wellington Citizens' Christmas Gift Fund, and by the Countess of Liverpool's Fund, Christchurch.

With such a fine nucleus, Mrs. Luke should be able to provide a first-rate dinner for the men. A sub-committee of ladies will make the puddings at the meat works at Ngahauranga, where they can be boiled with a minimum of trouble.

Trentham Camp

Dear Tom,

It's hard to believe that Christmas has already come and gone.

While many of the lads got leave to travel home there were still a good number who didn't. Most of the chaps from the South Island stayed put and I think there were around 3,000 of us in total. The Wellington Mayoress and ladies from the committee were determined we wouldn't suffer and the camp was decorated with ferns and palms and fresh green bushes.

I'd have to say, the food we had was fit for a king. Roast lamb, green peas and potatoes, followed by boiled plum duff for pud. But the highlight of the day was when they brought out two barrels of beer. The men swooped like vultures and the first one was emptied quick smart. But there was a problem with the bung from the second barrel and it wasn't long before one frustrated soldier attacked it with a screwdriver and hammer. You can imagine what happened next, Jack. The beer gushed out like a geyser soaking everyone in sight.

I trust you all had a quiet day at home. Wish I'd been there.

Much love,

Jack

Dear Jack,

Ha, ha! What a laugh!

Our Christmas day wasn't near as funny as that. It wasn't too bad though. Mrs J came over and helped Ma with the food. We had roast lamb as well — donated by Uncle Ced. And suet pudding for afters. Ma can't make plum duff but the suet pudding was okay.

For presents, Mrs J made Amy a doll. And I got a game called Ludo. We played it after lunch but there was no one good to play with.

It wasn't much fun having Christmas without you or our Dad.

Love from
Tom

Dear Tom,

Good news. It looks like we might be on the move
at last.

Some of the chaps in hut 29 have been told they
will sail out on the 10th. And a few mates in hut
21 have been drawn to go with them. I guess it's
only a matter of time now before the rest of us get
called.

Let's hope so.
Best regards,
Jack

NEW YEAR AT THE FRONT

GRIM SALUTE FROM BRITISH

SALVOS FROM ALL CALIBRES
SEND MISSILES INTO GERMAN
LINES.

The arrival of 1917 was welcomed on the Western front by the British and French soldiers as a beginning of the end of the great world war, says a despatch from a correspondent with the British armies in France. There may be varying views and theories as to how the end is to be brought about, but there is no question that throughout the British army there is a conviction that the next twelve months will bring a victorious peace to the Allies.

Opinion among the British and French fighters as to how the war will end is divided into two schools. The one believes that Germany will be willing to grant extreme concessions, and the other that only military pressure will bring the fruits of victory. Both schools are, however, agreed that this is the decisive year.

On most sectors of the British front the new year made its bow with little ceremony. So many flares and rockets are sent up from the trenches on these long, dark, winter nights that it was impossible to say how many of these on Sunday night were in honour of 1917. There is one sector, however, where the British artillery followed the practice adopted last year of welcoming 1st January with salvos against the enemy from guns of all calibres. Along this front everything from machine-guns to the biggest of the "heavies" joined in firing, first one round, then nine, then one, and finally six. "We do not know whether the Germans recognised it or not, but we will try them again to-night," said an artillery captain as he started for a distant part of the line to give the necessary instructions.

In sending this fiery greeting to the Germans there was a further complication of difference of time, the Germans observing Continental time, which is one hour ahead of the British and French clocks. To avoid all doubt the British artillery fired signal salvos at both 11 o'clock and midnight. Low, black clouds scudded over the battle area the last night of the old year, and its successor was borne in on a howling wind, which caught up and carried the thunder of the guns. The grim booming was swept far beyond the battle lines until it mingled with the church bells summoning the people to prayer in the war-bound villages of France.

January, 1917

Dear Jack,

Your good news was Ma's bad news. Ma has been in tears all week. I think she had her heart set on this war being over before you got on the troop-ship. Good old Mrs J came galloping to the rescue with four jars of jam to cheer us all up. She says her gooseberry bush is growing fruit faster than you can say 'Jack Robinson'. I think it was a good excuse to visit and she's probably just trying to keep an eye on Ma. She must be going through a lot of sugar though. And sugar's in short supply right now.

Everyone's doing what they can for the war effort. A few ladies from Ma's church group came round to ours on Tuesday. They were having a meeting about making things for the soldiers and by two o'clock our whole sitting room was full of ladies armed with knitting needles. They must have jabbered away for at least two hours.

Uncle Ced reckons they're noisier than a gaggle of geese. He says it's not a man's world any more. That's 'cause nearly all the men have gone away to war. Everyone except Uncle Ced, that is. And Mr Gilbertson, of course.

Hope all is good with you.

Lots of love,

From Tom

APPEAL TO WOMEN OF THE DOMINION.

Dear Tom,

Goodness gracious, mate. What's our world coming to, eh? Knitting needles, hats . . . seems like the whole world's turned upside down.

Give my regards to Mr Gilbertson and tell him to save me a pound of his best saveloys for when I get home.

Best regards,
Jack

Dear Jack,

We're back at school now. And I'm writing this letter in class because writing letters is easier than doing sums. I know how much you enjoy getting letters from home.

The Valley has had its share of bad news lately. Marian Murdoch's brother is home for good now and has to go everywhere in a wheelchair. Marian doesn't mention it much these days. When he came to church last week everyone stared. I felt so sorry for him. You wouldn't recognise him Jack, because his hair has turned completely white.

Mrs Stains' brother had to come home from the war as well. He's only got half an arm on his right side but at least he doesn't have to go everywhere in a wheelchair.

In church on Sunday the vicar made us say a special prayer for all our brave soldiers. He even said your name, Jack. Private Jack Donald William McAllister. It gave me goosebumps to hear your name called out like that, with you being so far away and everything.

It's been a long time and soon I'll start forgetting what you look like. I hope your hair doesn't go white like Marian's brother, but Mrs J said if it does she's got the perfect remedy. It's got something to do with lavender flowers.

Yesterday Mrs Stains gave us a rousing speech about how well the New Zealand soldiers are doing and how they have a perfect fighting record. She said the kiwis and the Aussies are the best soldiers out. Go the ANZACs! I told her you were off on the troop-ship any minute now and she said she'd say a prayer for your safe return.

Love from Tom

Dear Tom,

My hair is still a fine shade of mousey brown, as far as I can tell, but I'll keep lavender flowers in mind should the situation change. It's good to know I'm in your thoughts and it's reassuring to be well prayed for because it looks like things are finally moving.

I think we'll be needing all the help we can get. We've been issued with our sea kits now — a hold-all, a mess dish and a new uniform, which includes a waist belt, hat and a new pair of boots. Three thousand soldiers were inspected by officers before getting marched off to our huts. It must have been quite a sight. Army life is getting serious. There's not so much larking about and the training schedule has stepped up a notch. Last Saturday's route march took all day. The wind was blowing like blazes and I was fair tuckered out by the finish.

They say our troop-ship is scheduled to leave in ten days' time. I don't know full details but it looks like there will be a few hundred on board. Fingers crossed I don't get seasick because it's going to be a long hard six weeks if I do.

Best regards,
Jack

Dear Jack,

I guess by now you will be on board the troop-ship.

Ma said to tell you she's sorry we couldn't come and see you off. It was too far to go in the finish, and would have cost too much money. I think it's probably just as well we didn't go because Ma would have only ended up crying her eyes out.

Poor Ma. She bursts into tears a lot these days and tries to blame her crying on the onions. Trouble is, we don't have too many onions left. Uncle Ced brought some round. They were from his garden but they have to hang in the shed till they dry out properly. Another six months, he reckons. Hopefully they'll be ready for when you get home, Jack.

Anyway, enough about us. What about you? Fancy being on a ship, eh. What's it like? Have you seen any whales yet? Or sharks?

I hope you have a good voyage and don't forget to write when you get the chance.

Lots of love,

From Tom

PS — I've been practising my sketches. This is one Amy did of her and me waving.

And this is one of an elephant. If your zoo-keeper is right about elephants being good luck then you'll probably need as many as you can get.

On board a troop-ship

Dear Tom,

That was a great sketch, mate. The ears were a fine shape and you got the shading just right. I liked young Amy's drawing too.

A lot has happened since I last wrote and, yes, we are on the high seas at last.

There was a huge crowd in Wellington to see us off and it was a rousing sight with music, flags and brass bands to boot. The ship is enormous and climbing aboard with everyone cheering made me feel like the King himself.

I will write again soon.

Love,

Jack

Dear Tom,

So many miles away now and land is but a distant memory. I think it might take some getting used to, this new life at sea. I'm feeling a bit crook in the guts already, and I must say, not having my feet on dry land is the oddest feeling in the world. Hopefully things will settle down with time.

You'll be pleased to know that writing letters isn't going to be a problem. The authorities say we can continue sending mail home and it will be collected from ports along the way. You might even get some new stamps for your collection. Arnold says there are some special war editions out.

And I'm pleased to report the old gang is still hanging together. Billy and I have ended up as close neighbours. Colin Croft and Arnold Wilson aren't too far away, either.

I reckon it's just as well I didn't join the navy, Tom, because I'm definitely not cut out to be a sailor. I spend a good deal of my time barfing over the side and the next few weeks might turn out to be even tougher than Trentham.

They haven't eased up on the discipline, either. We have four compulsory drills per day and all duties have to be performed like clockwork. The domestic duties can be challenging as well.

We wash our clothes in salt water, with no soap, and the quartermaster inspects the cleaning every day. He's a pedantic little man called Irwin who used to manage a haberdashery shop in South Dunedin. He's got a sharp little grey moustache and a sharp little personality to match.

Getting a good night's sleep isn't the easiest for run-of-the-mill soldiers like us. It's only the officers who have the luxury of a cabin. The rest of us are crammed together in the hold where there's not much room for tossing and turning. A quiet night's rest is usually out of the question with the ship's propeller banging away like blazes all night long!

On the bright side, the tucker isn't too bad. Last night we had soup, smoked fish and apples. Must go for now.

Love to all,

Your brother, Jack

PS — We haven't seen a whale yet but yesterday a school of dolphins followed our ship for a good couple of hours.

Dear Jack,

Dolphins, eh. Jeepers!

I wish I could have lessons in a ship with dolphins following along behind. School isn't too much fun just now, Jack. Don't tell Ma, but I got 'six of the best' from the headmaster last week. It's a long story, and even though it wasn't my fault, I ended up copping most of the blame. Still stings like billy-o.

I've got seventeen stamps in my collection now. Richard McGregor swapped me one of his favourites. It's got a picture of a bird on it and it came all the way from England! I'm looking forward to getting more from overseas soon. It seems like ages since I got your last letter … and even longer since I saw you.

You'll be pleased to hear that our Jacky's growing bigger every day. He can chew proper beef bones now and Mr Gilbertson saves him lamb shanks too, 'cause he's got exotic tastes and doesn't like savs. He also likes to finish off the morning porridge, which suits Amy because she's always looking for excuses not to finish hers.

Uncle Ced reckons Jacky's got plenty of brains for a dog and he's pretty cunning too.

We've almost stopped him peeing inside. There've only been a few accidents so far but they were mostly our Amy's fault because she snuck him into her bed. Amy is such a soft touch and doesn't like the thought of dogs sleeping outside. Too bad if he's got fleas though, eh.

Speaking of fleas — Ma said to tell you to keep up your hygiene standards and don't forget to say your prayers.

But Mrs J said what good are prayers when all anyone wants to do is kill each other. Ma got her pursed lips going when she said that. 'We need prayers more than ever these days, Nola,' she said. 'And I'm damned if I'm going to let this war turn me into a heathen.'

Love from

Tom

Private Frederick John Morey, killed in action on October 12, was the second son of Mrs E. O'Connor, of the Village Settlement, Rakaia. He was under 20 years of age when he left New Zealand with the Third Reinforcements. On Gallipoli he was wounded in the left hand, and in Egypt he contracted enteric fever and received a sunstroke. He was invalided to England, and spent nearly 12 months, chiefly at Hornchurch, before entering the firing-line in France. He had just returned to duty from furlough when he was killed.

Private Albert Thomas Stephen, died of wounds on October 24, was the youngest son of the late Mr James Stephen, of Staveley, and a brother of Mrs G. Collard, of Rakaia. Private Stephen enlisted at the age of 18, but relatives secured his discharge from camp on account of his age. His determination was shown, however, in his enlisting again from the Taranaki district, under the name of B. T. Anderson, and this name appeared in the casualty list. He left with the Twentieth Reinforcements. He was born at Staveley, and attended the Springburn School, and was well known in the Mount Somers and Rakaia districts. At the time of his death he was only 19½ years of age.

Dear Tom,

Tell Ma there's no need to fret. War is not going to make heathens of anyone on this troop-ship. Not if Father O'Brien has anything to do with it. He's the chaplain on board and he takes a church service every day. The service takes place in the mess room, which is definitely not the most sacred place on God's earth, especially when it's full of men smoking cigarettes and playing poker.

Still . . . I reckon he does a pretty good job under the circumstances.

It's going to take a long while to get to England. There's a lot of ocean out there and until you make the voyage yourself you don't realise how far away our little country is.

I started thinking about our Dad's family the other day. It's only when you get on a ship like this that you appreciate how hard it must have been for the settlers who came out to New Zealand. It's a world away from bonny Scotland, that's for sure.

Best regards,

Jack

Dear Jack,

Speaking of bonny Scotland, Ma said to remind you about our Dad's folks coming from Aberdeen. She said our aunty and uncle still live there — that's Aunty Doris and Uncle Hugh. Aunty Doris is Dad's sister ... Ma thinks she's got the address somewhere among Dad's papers and it would be grand if you got a chance to visit them.

I don't know where Aberdeen is exactly. But there's a map of the world in our classroom and I can see exactly where Scotland is. It's right on top of England and underneath a place called the Shetland Isles. You're right about the UK being a long way off. You might just as well be headed for Mars.

Hey Jack! Guess what? Uncle Ced came round last Saturday to help build the kennel. He brought some timber and we used the old iron and the nails from the shed, just like you said. Amy wanted to help but she turned out to be more of a nuisance. So we put her on dog-sitting duty while Uncle Ced and I banged in nails.

Ma paid Uncle Ced with fresh eggs and girdle scones. After that he was 'happy as a sandboy' as our Dad used to say. You know how much Uncle Ced likes his tucker, 'specially Ma's girdle scones.

School is hard this year, Jack. We have to do arithmetic, composition and geography every day. And then we have exams. I still reckon I'd be more use at home chopping wood.

Hope you are well.

Love from

Tom

Dear Tom,

Hang in there, mate. Study hard and always do your best. Make the old North East Valley School proud. That's what our Dad would have wanted. Ma will be pleased as punch if you do well.

Seems there's no escaping school work, eh — not even here on the high seas. Some of the lads are doing some study to pass the time. Billy put his name down for French the other day. And a couple of other lads are doing engineering papers. It's good to have something to do in your spare time besides playing poker, which usually just leads to punch ups.

Best regards,
Your brother, Jack

PS — Our Crofty got himself in a bit of strife last week. He's a good cards player when he puts his mind to it and the chap he was playing wasn't too sharp. So the chap finished up losing his hand and a few days' wages as well.

Things got heated when Crofty demanded his winnings and it took a few of the lads stepping in to prevent an all-out brawl.

Dear Jack,

Can you teach me how to play poker when you get home? Then we could have a game together. Ma and Mrs J play sometimes but they never get round to showing me how. Usually I end up playing patience by myself or draughts with Amy. I found our Dad's draughts set in the top cupboard last week and I've been teaching Amy how to play. There were two black pieces missing but I found some coat buttons in Ma's sewing kit that did the trick.

I'm not one for indoor games anyway. I'd rather be outside, especially when the weather's good.

Frank and I caught some lobbies in Lindsay Creek on Sunday arvo. We took off on one of the old cycles from the shed. I was doubling him at the start but he's getting a big lad and we soon ditched the bike near Chingford Park and walked the rest of the way.

We took the tin bucket from our shed and one of Ma's old dishcloths for a net. Ma said she supposed it was safer catching lobbies than shooting rabbits. Luckily she hadn't seen our creek for a while or she wouldn't have let us go anywhere near it. There's been a heap of rain lately and it's the highest I've seen it for ages.

Anyway, we were walking along minding our own business when, guess who we ran into? Harold Duncan and his dodgy mate, Eric. Remember him? I think you were pals with his brother, Albie. Harold's nothing like Albie. Harold's a proper bully. They were waiting for us when we got back to the bike. And they threatened to knock our blocks off if we didn't hand over the lobbies.

We didn't argue on account of Harold Duncan being built like a brick lavvy. No one argues with Harold Duncan. He's got fat knees and he smells like old socks. He's got a firecracker temper as well.

Even so, I don't reckon he'd have pushed us round if you'd been about, Jack. You'd have shown him!

Love from

Tom

PS — This is a drawing of me with the lobbies — before they got stolen.

Dear Tom,

You tell that Harold Duncan — any more of his nonsense and he'll have me to answer to. God knows how much I hate bullies. That's why we have to fight this war in the first place — because of bullies. Joves, Tom. Don't get me started.

Just stand your ground and don't back down. If you show any sign of weakness you're done for. That's what they tell us in the army, anyway. Not that we've had a chance to put it into practice yet. We had a much needed change of scenery yesterday when we went through a canal. Amazing! The first stretch is through flat marshy land, which is well built up and planted in trees. Then you go through locks, 1000 feet long and 110 feet wide!

The whole canal is quite a feat of engineering and an incredible sight to see. There are electric engines to the side that pull the ship through and after the first gates close the water comes racing in — raising the ship until the lock's full. (These gates are seven feet thick!) Once you get between the high walls the gates close again until the water raises the ship level. It takes around six hours to pass through the entire canal, which gave us something new to talk about at least. It's easy to get sick of the same thing, day after day. Boredom is hard to live with and it doesn't take much for the lads to get tetchy, especially with no shore leave yet.

Some of us have been busy putting together a magazine. It's called 'From Maoriland to Blighty' and it should make a first-class read. I got talked into doing a few sketches and I wrote a poem as well. The poem was all about our Dad and it's got some good rhymes. Stampy's effort was first-class. He's got quite a way with words when he sets his mind to it. I'll send you a copy when it's done.

Well, that's about all for now, Tom. We've been told the mail closes in the morning, so there must be a port coming up. Let's hope we get some leave this time.

I hope you're looking after Ma and Amy, and keeping the home fires burning.

Best regards,
Your brother,
Jack

Dear Jack,

Don't worry. The home fires will be burning away fine this winter, thanks to Uncle Ced.

He felled a bluegum tree last weekend and we spent the whole day axing it into blocks. The wood is green as grass just now but Uncle Ced reckons six months in the woodshed should dry it out okay.

Hey! Guess what our Jacky did last week? The little beggar ran away. Usually he doesn't go far but this time I left the gate open and we didn't notice him missing till it was too late.

What a job we had getting him home again. He ran for miles and so did we — all the way down past the shops and up Opoho Road. We ended up with half the neighbourhood out looking and finally found the little rascal asleep in Mrs Ramsay's wash house. Amy was pretty upset and I don't think Ma was too happy either.

It gave me a real fright and I got to thinking how sad it would be if we lost Jacky before you two got the chance to meet.

I haven't let him out of my sight since.

Lots of love,

Tom

PS — This drawing is supposed to be our Jacky but I'm afraid dogs aren't my strong point.

Somewhere out at sea

Dear Tom,

I liked your drawing, mate. It showed good composition and, with a bit of extra shading, it would make a top-class sketch. I could do with some new pencils out here but seems they're scarce as hen's teeth. If you send another parcel would you mind putting in a couple? Also, some of Ma's shortbread wouldn't go amiss. The last lot travelled well and it was the best thing I've eaten in a long while.

Joves, Tom. Sometimes this voyage feels like it's never going to end. Tension continues to build on board and the boys are going stir-crazy with no shore leave granted.

We pulled in at a coaling wharf yesterday and were told we were going to be allowed off the ship. But the beggars changed their minds at the last minute and wouldn't let anyone off, which didn't go down well.

I reckon they'll be lucky not to have a mutiny on their hands soon. We've all been cooped up like chooks for so long that the strain's starting to show. Some of these lads are loose cannons at the best of times. There's one bloke by the name of Ricketts who likes to pick on the younger ones. Yesterday Thomas Bathgate had just about had enough and there was a bit of a dust up. Alfred

Hoffman stepped in and threatened to knock Ricketts' block off on his behalf. It all got out of hand and there were punches flying left, right and centre.

When the Sarge got wind of it he put the soldiers involved on report and gave the rest of us yet another lecture.

'Look here lads,' he said. 'It's the Germans we've come to fight, not each other.'

But you can't keep the troops all cooped up like chickens and not expect a few feathers to fly, eh.

Best regards,

Jack

Dear Private Jack McAllister,

Chickens! Ha! I know just what you mean. Chickens are what made our Jacky run away. I found that out when I caught him with a mouth full of feathers last week. I only just managed to hide them in my pockets before anyone saw. Poor Jacky'd cop a bullet if he got found out. I'll have to train that out of him, quick smart.

So what else's been happening? Not much.

School is pretty much the same as usual. Boring sonnets and sums I can't do. This week we have to write poems about summer, using 'interesting adjectives'. That means 'rolling' meadows and 'babbling' brooks. But you know me, Jack. I don't see the point in writing la-di-da poems about stuff like that. And who's ever heard of a babbling brook in North East Valley anyway? Lindsay Creek doesn't babble. Only Mrs Baxter babbles. She's our new Sunday school teacher. She also keeps bees.

Frank Morrison's good at poems. He wrote a cracker one about the war. Arthur Mitchell drew a picture instead. He drew soldiers shot to pieces on a battlefield. It was quite bloodthirsty and Mrs Stains looked upset. She said she hoped they weren't New Zealand soldiers and Arthur said he didn't know what kind of soldiers they were yet, he was still deciding.

We do lots of war things these days. Mrs Stains made us draw flags last week. We had to draw Great Britain and France and Russia and then we had a go at Australia and New Zealand. Most of us didn't know the difference.

But if you didn't get them right you had to stand in the

corridor until you remembered. Harold Duncan got his wrong and had to sing *God Save the King* all by himself in assembly.

I didn't feel sorry for him in the least!

Lots of love,

From Tom

Dear Jack,

I haven't heard from you in a while so thought I'd write again even though it's not my turn.

Guess what?! Ma is teaching me how to knit. I'm going to knit scarves for the soldiers. Well, maybe not all of them, just one or two. Ma said if I could only sit still for five minutes she'd show me what to do. It took longer than five minutes, but I think I'm starting to get the hang of it.

Knitting is harder than you think, Jack. It's a tricky business because you have to do three things at the same time. Like holding your needles the right way and making sure you don't get your counting wrong. It pays to have your tongue in the right place as well, according to Mrs J. And it doesn't help to have fingers sticky with jam.

Mrs J says not to worry because practice makes perfect. I will try and get my first scarf knitted for your birthday, Jack. That's not far away now, eh. What will you do to celebrate? Mrs J is coming over to our house and we're going to have some cake in your honour. I hope it's chocolate but I've got a feeling it might be sultana on account of the cocoa shortage.

Lots of love
From Tom

Still somewhere at sea

Dear Tom,

Sorry I haven't written lately. There's been no mail to speak of in ages.

Blimey! I'd almost forgotten my own birthday. There's not much celebrating to be done here, I'm afraid. I look forward to receiving your scarf though. Good on you mate, and keep up the good work. There are loads of soldiers who would be glad of a nice warm scarf just now because it's brass monkey weather out here. Recently two signallers on the bridge got frostbite on their toes.

The low temperatures take some getting used to. Last week when I was on submarine duty the wind chill was minus ten. We only do half-hour shifts in temperatures like that because it's too cold to go any longer. We do half on–half off, with a warm-up time in-between. Our duties last for twelve hours so we're dead on our feet by the end of it.

16 days later:

Hallelujah, Tom! We've been told our next stop will be Scotland or England. I don't mind which. All I know is, I won't be sorry to see the back end of this boat. Tell Ma I'll send a postcard when I can.

Best regards,
Jack

Dear Jack,

Happy birthday to you. Happy birthday to you.
   Happy birthday dear J-a-a-ck. Happy birthday to you.
Hip hip hooray!

As a special treat Ma put a tin of honey in her last parcel — it's clover honey from Mrs Baxter's hives and I hope it arrives in good condition. Ma put in some cocoa as well, courtesy of good old Mrs J.

I hope you got my scarf in the parcel. You'll notice a few holes that aren't supposed to be there but, with a bit of luck, the next one should be much improved.

Ma is knitting like crazy these days. And so is Mrs J. Last week they both nearly ran out of wool. It was panic stations with Mrs Wilson coming to the rescue with emergency supplies. Mrs Wilson is the new lady from church. She brings us old jumpers that we have to unpick and make into new things for the soldiers.

Lots of love,
From Tom

PS — Did you find the little wooden elephant in your parcel? I got it at the church jumble and thought you might like to wear it round your neck for luck.

Dear Tom,

Thanks a lot for the parcel. It was waiting for me when the boat finally docked. I'm pleased to report the honey travelled with minimal leakage and the cocoa was much appreciated.

We reached our destination at 9pm but weren't allowed off the ship until the next morning. By that time everyone was breaking their necks to have a look around but we had to obey orders and stay put. We finally boarded a train just before midday.

Crikey, Tom. There's so much to see and I've been making lots of notes in my sketchbook. The countryside is very different to New Zealand. The farms are more orderly for a start — neatly laid out and square with hedge borders. Also, most of the animals live in barns here. Can you imagine herding kiwi cows into barns? I'm sure there'd be an uprising — from livestock and farmers alike. Of course, there are sheep here in England too, but not in the numbers we see back home.

We've seen a few new places already. We passed over the canal to Manchester, then on to Crewe, Stafford, Wolverhampton, Birmingham, Banbury and Oxford. The names are interesting and some are even familiar. I've heard them talk of Brighton and Portobello. Don't know if they'll be anything like our Brighton and Portobello, though. And I have no idea when, or if, I'll get to visit them.

It was pitch dark when we reached Banbury so we headed straight for Sling Camp. Our new home is in Wiltshire, on Salisbury Plain, which is seventy-four miles south-west of London. It's a bit like Saddle Hill to look at but feels very different to Trentham. I don't know what to make of the place yet. Khaki brown tents for as far as the eye can see.

One thing's for sure, we're in the real army now, Tom. No doubt about it. There's even more saluting and drilling than before. The rules are strict and we've been told we could be here for a while so we better get used to it. It's feeling a lot like winter and I haven't seen snow on the ground like this in a long while. Thinking of you all back home.

Give my love to everyone.

Best regards,

Jack

Dear Jack,

I'm glad you finally made it safe and sound to England. There have been some awful stories going round about soldiers perishing at sea. Imagine going off to war and dying before you even got there! Ma said it doesn't bear thinking about.

The telegram man has been coming to our neighbourhood more regularly lately and we all dread the sight of him. Yesterday he came down North Road just after lunch. We could see him pedalling round the corner from the bedroom window. Ma was sure he was going to stop at our place because he slowed right down. It looked like he was getting off his bike near our gate and we thought something had happened to you. Ma got me all worked up and in the end I could hardly breathe because my chest hurt so much.

Thank goodness he was only fixing his chain and, lucky for us, he carried on past. Not so lucky for the Carson's though. We found out the next day he stopped at theirs.

James Carson died from wounds he got in France. His name will be in the newspaper in the roll of honour.

Love from

Tom

ROLL OF HONOUR.

TO-DAY'S CASUALTY LIST.

Reported Killed in Action.

Anderson, M.
Richmond, W. O.
Page, R. D.
Macdonald, W. C.
Baillie, F.
Day, L. A. H.
Farquharson, T. M.
Hunter, C.
Parkyn, L.
Searchfield, T.
McKenzie, H.
Baldwin, S. H.
McGowan, W. J.
Robertson, E. H.
Schumacher, G. J.
Baker, J. R.
Belton, E. L.
Dennison, J. A.
Jurnett, T. H.
Alley, J.
Harding, G. F.
Hillier, A. L.
Leslie, J. F.
Pickering, G.
Aidley, J. W.
Shepherd, H. G.
Tattersall, W. J.
Cunningham, W. J.
Davidson, L. L.

Correction.

Previously reported missing, now reported killed in action:

Birss, A. C., Second-Lieutenant.

Previously reported missing, believed wounded, now declared by Court of Enquiry killed in action:

Rifleman J. S. Black
Rifleman A. Fleming
Rifleman H. Smith

The following reported missing, believed killed:

Private L. M. Newlove
Rifleman E. C. Brown
Rifleman J. McKechnie
Rifleman A. C. Stevens

Previously reported killed in action October 17, now reported admitted to hospital, October 18, dangerously ill:

Private W. J. Kroon.

Reported Died of Wounds.

Sapper T. J. McMahon
Private E. A. Mason
Gunner R. Lee
Gunner W. J. Tielle
Gunner J. Carson
Private D. Barns
Rifleman A. B. McCorkingale

The following reported died of sickness:

Private D. J. Walker

Continued from previous page:

The following reported wounded:
Private R. F. Hanan, Private J. H.
Hislop, Driver L. W. Hopkins, Private
H. Butterworth, Corporal W. Hamil-
ton, Private Journeaux, Private J.
McGowan, Private T. P. Smith, Pri-
vate L. Weir, Private A. F. Atkinson,
Gunner R. T. Beveridge, Gunner T.
G. Madden, Gunner D. A. Kemp, Gun-
ner P. Lock, Driver A. Wilson, Gun-
ner A. L. Harris, Driver F. Ward,
Driver W. Scott, Bombardier E. N.
C. Clarkson, Gunner J. Dryden, Gun-
ner K. M. Forsyth, Gunner C. Gibson,
Gunner H. E. Goldsbro, Corporal T.
Kirton, Gunner W. J. Randle, Gunner
J. A. H. Vivian, Gunner F. R. Wood,
Gunner W. S. Terry, Gunner W. M.
Sutherland, Corporal H. R. Hill, Pri-
vate T. Simn, Private J. Land, Private
J. Parks, Private S. P. Pegler,
Private A. T. Prince, Private G. A.
Underwood, Private F. Hurley, Lance-
Corporal W. G. Brown, Private A. J.
Milford, Private F. E. Carter, Corporal
R. Chisholm, Private M. J. Enright,
Lance-Corporal W. A. Hughes, Pri-
vate C. Q. Robinson, Lance-Corporal
S. P. Robertson, Lance-Corporal J.
Taylor, Lance-Corporal S. G. Taylor,
Private T. Vickers, Private W. C.
Guy, Private R. Ifwersen, Corporal
W. F. Mahoney, Private C. M. Bau-
erle, Private R. M. Becroft, Lance-
Corporal T. W. Chitty, Lance-Corporal
A. McKenzie, Private R. V. Mc-
Veigh, Private E. Morris, Private E.
E. A. Pailthorpe.

Dear Tom,

I received another of your parcels today. Please thank Ma for the shortbread and tell her it was a great treat to get the butter. Also, many thanks for the elephant, which I'm going to keep in my trouser pocket for luck.

Things are pretty grim in England just now. The bad news from the Front continues and the casualty lists are worse than expected. Thousands of men are perishing daily and there's no sign of it letting up.

The Somme had such heavy losses last year and apparently men are still dying in hospital from wounds they got there. Everyone's been knocked for a six by the scale of things. And I don't think anyone really knows what'll happen next.

I miss you all a lot.

Give Amy and Ma a hug for me.

Much love,

Jack

Dear Jack,

We are thinking about you all the time these days.

Yesterday I climbed to the top branch of the plum tree down behind the shed. You can see for miles from up there because it's grown even higher than ever. Remember when you used to take your cobbers up after school? You let me come with you once and we sat and talked and ate so many plums that our lips turned purple.

Anyway — I stayed up there for ages yesterday, just thinking. Mrs J says too much thinking can make you melancholy. I'm not sure what melancholy is exactly but it doesn't sound like much fun.

This week Mrs J told us we all have to be cheerful. She said if we think good thoughts then good things will happen. She even brought Ma some daisies to cheer her up.

What sort of flowers do they have in England, Jack?

Marian Murdoch says they have mostly roses. She knows all about England on account of her mother being born there, and also because of her brother being in hospital there too. England looks quite small on the map. Even smaller than New Zealand. I wonder what the people are like.

Marian says they talk funny. She says the English are prim and proper with a stiff upper lip.

Love from

Tom

Sling Camp, Wiltshire

Dear Tom,

I think Marian Murdoch is referring to the English reputation for a stiff upper lip, which means they like to keep their emotions under the surface. I've noticed they like things done more formally than we do and they have a few different customs as well.

From what I've seen, Englishmen may take some getting to know. They are quite reserved and seem to regard us 'diggers' as a bit rough round the edges. That's probably because we don't take kindly to all their bowing and scraping. And we don't like being bossed around either!

Still . . . I reckon there's not too much difference underneath. At the end of the day we've all got ten fingers and ten toes. (Well, we did before we came here, anyway!)

Best regards,
Jack

PS — 'Melancholy' means sad and gloomy. I guess it's what people get like when they think too much about sad things. Poor Ma.

Dear Jack,

Guess what?

Uncle Ced chopped more firewood last week. I helped him stack it in the shed. He says we should have enough to see us through next winter, providing we don't go silly with it. No chance of that these days with Ma refusing to light the fire in the sitting room till you get back. She thinks it'll bring us bad luck for some reason.

I loved the stamp you put on your last letter, Jack. But I've got two of them already so I swapped it with Frank for a green halfpenny one with the word 'Victorialand' on it.

Better go now and start chopping wood before Ma starts nagging.

Take care big brother.

Lots of love,

Tom

PS — Amy says to say hello. She can print her name all by herself now. She's neater than me with a pencil, and Ma says I better get cracking 'cause she's good at her times tables too.

PPS — In your next letter can you tell me more about Sling Camp, Jack.

Sling Camp

Dear Tom,

I'm glad you liked the stamp and managed to find a good use for it.

Sling Camp, eh. Well, what can I say? It's not a place you'd want to come for your holidays, if that's what you're thinking. We were all given stern lectures on arrival. And they told us we have thirty days to be 'knocked into shape' and turned into 'proper' soldiers. (Whatever that means!)

The food is well below Trentham standards and the accommodation isn't much better. From where I'm standing I can see rows and rows of khaki tents. They are all very orderly and organised but the place is pretty bleak. Everyone wears the same colour clothes and the Sergeant-major shouts out orders every minute of the day.

Speaking of which, I can hear someone bellowing in the distance as I write.

Better sign off for now and go jump to attention.

Best regards,

Your brother, Jack

Dear Jack,

Sorry I haven't written in a while. Ma has been laid low with 'flu. She didn't want me telling you about it till she was well on the mend. She's been crook for a few weeks now. The doctor had to visit twice and then Aunty Jean came to look after us. You know what Aunty Jean's like — a total killjoy. If there's any fun to be had she'll squash it in a flash.

I was so glad when she left, Jack. She wouldn't let me go near the plum tree in case I fell out. She's even stricter than Ma and not so tender-hearted. That's what Uncle Cedric says. It's hard to think of them as sisters. I wonder what they were like as kids. I bet Aunty Jean was the bossy one. And I bet Ma didn't get a word in edgewise.

Poor Jacky wasn't allowed in the house the whole time Aunty Jean was here and even the fowls went off the lay in the finish. Things are better now though, with Ma up and moving again.

I'm so pleased I didn't get the 'flu. I hate being poorly. And I can't stand lying about in bed all day, either. Last month I had a day off school with a crook stomach and I got fed up with staring at the walls after five minutes.

So, what else's been happening? Oh, yeah . . . Uncle Ced came on Saturday. He'd been pig hunting with Uncle Keith and they stuck a boar somewhere up near Mount Cargill. Everyone was pretty excited and we had dinner together to celebrate. Even Mrs J was invited. She brought round a huge pot of vegie soup. It would have been nicer without all the silver beet though. Mrs J says silver beet is good for your blood. I think a person's blood can do fine on its own.

Speaking of blood, I might be going rabbit shooting again next week. Sure hope so.

Lots of love,

From Tom

PS — Guess what? Mrs Stains was telling us the reason why the seasons in England are opposite to New Zealand. She said it's all because of the earth and the sun. She tried to explain using an apple for the earth and a plum from Marian's lunchbox for the sun. I didn't quite get it and I still can't imagine what it'd be like having Christmas in the wintertime. But I bet you'll be glad to come home and have proper seasons again.

Sling Camp

Dear Tom,

It's good to know you're holding the fort, mate. Ma is lucky to have you and you are lucky to have her. Look after each other, and Amy. I know you'll do your best, Tom. You're a good lad and I couldn't ask for a better brother.

What a lark we're going to have when I get back home, eh. I can't wait. And I'm really looking forward to meeting our Jacky.

I wonder how many people are allowed on an elephant at once. What a treat it's going to be.

I had a dream last night. I was at home helping our Dad fix up the shed and I was all set to nail the iron in place when Crofty's snoring woke me up. (That's when it turned into a nightmare!)

Seriously, Tom. I think I'd give my right arm for a few days back in kiwiland right now. The British soldiers get home leave but New Zealand is a bit far away for such luxury.

Still, we make an effort to make the most of any time off, even if it's just a few hours. On Sunday we managed to get over the hill for a walk and we treated ourselves to a feed at an inn. It was a quaint old place with shutters on the windows and a fair dinkum thatched roof.

The food wasn't too badly priced either. Eggs, bread and a slice of vanilla cake for two shillings, which is pretty good value when you consider our wages here are five shillings a day. That's four shillings more than the British soldiers get and a shilling less than the Australians.

Unfortunately, there hasn't been much opportunity for sightseeing yet.

The routine is fairly tedious and humdrum. War isn't at all like you'd expect. And so far it hasn't been in the least exciting. Most days are full up with marches and drills. Every day we rise at six and we train for several hours. The morning parade is at 7:40am — followed by a stiff inspection by the platoon commander. Half an hour later there's a battalion parade.

It's all very traditional and army hierarchy reigns supreme. Privates like us don't get much respect over here and we're all expected to know our place. Usually we get spoken to like a pack of schoolboys by a regimental Sergeant-major called Cunningham. He's a fierce little ginger bloke who likes to throw his weight about and makes our Sergeant Harvey look like a pussycat.

The officers at Sling are what Mrs J would call 'stick-in-the-mud' and everything runs with clockwork precision. Your kit has to be polished to within an inch of its life. And boots, belt, rifle and pack must all be spick and span. Or else! You don't want to know about 'or else', Tom. Suffice to say, we spend a lot of time saluting and drilling. And it pays to do everything right if you don't want to find yourself with all privileges removed and confined to barracks! On the positive side we are learning practical skills that might come in useful back home. Yesterday we had an extra drill in the afternoon and learned how to cut and repair the wire. I reckon I'd be able to have a fair crack at making a fence now. And, when we were done with that, we had a lesson in throwing grenades (not quite so practical, but necessary, nonetheless).

There's another bomb we're learning to use now. It's called the Mills bomb. They say if you get the action right, you should be able to hurl it ninety feet. I wouldn't like to be on the receiving end of one, that's for sure.

Best regards,

Your brother, Jack

PS — This is a sketch of me, making a fence.

Dear Private McAllister,

We could do with a few Mills bombs here just now, I reckon. Ammunition is hard to come by these days and I didn't shoot a single rabbit last time I went out with Uncle Ced. I guess the ammo's all earmarked for Europe.

Glad to hear you are picking up a few extra skills. It'd be good if you could fix up the boundary fences when you get back though. That'd be a real help.

Have you been to the frontline yet, Jack? Marian's brother said there are rats in the trenches. Big ones, the size of cats. And mud up to your eyeballs. And mice as well. Marian said there are lice that live on your body and in your hair and people get shot and left to die in the mud. That's what nearly happened to her brother — the one who had his leg blown off. Her brother went to Egypt as well. That's where the pyramids are. I think they've got camels too. Marian said the heat in Egypt was unbearable. Even worse than the Ida Valley in the heat of summer.

We had some bad news here last week. Owen Watson from the corner shop got killed and his family had to close the shop. He got killed at the frontline after a German sniper got him. He's the second brother to get shot. We had a service at church with egg sandwiches and orange cordial for afters.

Blimey! Those snipers sound dangerous, Jack. I haven't seen much of them on the news reels at the cinema though. I've only seen the soldiers from our side.

Lots of love,

Tom

PS — Do they have any rabbits in England?

Dear Tom,

I haven't been to the frontline yet, mate.

Most divisions spend around a week there at a time and I dare say my turn won't be too far off. I can't say I'm looking forward to it but reckon I'd rather be doing something more useful than endless army drills and route marches.

I'd be lying if I said I wasn't a bit scared though. They say that no amount of training prepares you for the Front and it doesn't come with too many positive recommendations.

The lads who've been there don't say much but I've heard they don't look too good when they get back. They say it's not a place you'd want to go if you didn't have to, put it that way. But don't worry, Tom. The McAllisters are made of stern stuff and I'll do my darndest to make it home in one piece. You can count on that.

Greetings from the Northern Hemisphere.

We're getting closer to action time now, Tom, and I've learned a lot more about what to expect at the Front. Frontline fighting takes place in trenches and the system is quite complex. Trenches are like ditches surrounded by masses of barbed wire. They go for miles on end with the no-man's-land area in the middle. These trenches take a lot of digging and the ANZACs have done their fair share of it. That's why we're called 'diggers'.

Apparently, if you want to stay alive you need to stay down low for as long as you can. If an attack is ordered you have to go forward. Going forward is also called 'going over the top'. And your job is to take as many Germans as possible before taking over their trenches.

Of course, the infantry are the ones who cop it first. We're the little guys with the most to lose. The big guns behind us send out the barrage. And if the barrage goes well the enemy soldiers are killed (theoretically, their barbed wire should get broken by exploding shells).

By gaining ground, yard by yard, we are supposed to win the war. It's a bit like a game of chess and the Generals move us around like pawns.

Billy said we should think of it like rugby. He said it's all about territory and possession. If the forwards do a proper job, the backs just need to pick up the ball and run. But if the forwards don't do their job properly, the infantry end up facing all the enemy tackles. Let's hope the artillery do their job right, that's all I can say.

Three days later:

No action yet, Tom, and, mercifully, the frontline is still a good way off.

Of course they're not letting us stand idle with route marches scheduled daily. Saturday morning is spent on fatigues and there's always a game of something in the afternoon. A few teams have been picked for football and hockey but most of my mates prefer the cross-country. I'm still keen on the three-mile race and, with all this training, I'm fitter than I've ever been. Not carrying too much extra weight these days, either.

Oh well . . . the Sarge is hovering so I'll keep my letter short and sweet this time.

Best regards

Your brother, Jack

PS — Stampy sends his regards.

Dear Jack,

We are having races at school too. Last week I got fourth
in the 100-yard dash. I always come fourth when it's 100
yards. I like longer races best (the half-mile especially)
but Frank Morrison prefers them short. He can run as
fast as anything for 100 yards, but he slows down pretty
quick at the end. He doesn't have the build for distance.
Not like me.

Uncle Ced says I'm like a wily old fox. Maybe I am. I
know I can walk for miles on a rabbit hunt. Last week, me
and Uncle Ced went right up to the top of Flagstaff and
across to Swampy Summit. We stayed there for most of
the day and cooked pork sausages on the fire for lunch.
They tasted great, even the burnt ones. Uncle Ced's going
to show me how to make damper next time, with flour
and water. I hope he comes again next weekend.

Lots of love,
From Tom

PS — In the cross-country Frank Morrison and Theo
Bathgate were battling it out for first and second. The
whole school was cheering when Frank passed Theo and
then Theo passed Frank about halfway and then Frank
passed Theo again just near the finish. Frank got first in the
end, but only by a hare's whisker. I've made a drawing of it.

PPS — Last night Mrs J came round to check us all for
worms. And not the kind you take fishing, either! She had
us all lined up outside the lavvy door.

Dear Tom,

That's a great picture, mate. I'm glad you and Uncle Ced are getting along so well these days. And I'm pleased you've stuck with your running too.

We had a trial run on the sports track recently — it was a three-mile teams' race. Each team had nine men and the six fastest times got tallied up at the end.

Some of the chaps put in some good performances. I didn't go so well myself this time because the course was steep and slippery and I've got a bit of a bad throat. I hope I'm not coming down with anything, though it wouldn't be surprising considering what's going on down here.

The camp's been hit hard with 'flu and measles and they've isolated some of the huts to stop it spreading. The odd thing is, they've got us eating and sleeping separately but they still make us do our drills together. I'm not sure how effective the isolation will be as there've been reports of some soldiers dying from 'flu already. It's something you want to keep your distance from, that's for sure.

Best regards,

Your brother, Jack

Dear Jack,

I hope you don't come down with 'flu or measles.

 Ma said to keep warm and dry and get some medicine into you. She asked if you needed more honey? Lemons are good too, Ma said. I wonder if they grow lemons in England? Last year Amy and I made lemonade — we tried to sell it down at the front gate — do you remember?

 Love from

 Tom

PS — I've done a sketch to try and cheer you up. It's our Jacky catching a ball. Good, eh.

PPS — Mrs J says if you have any trouble with your lungs we can always send a bottle of Baxter's.

Dear Tom,

Ha! Yes! I remember the lemonade. I think you used up all Ma's sugar and she wasn't best pleased. I could do with a glass of it now, to be honest. I reckon that would just about do the trick.

There's not too much medicine to be had here. And I don't think I've seen a lemon since I left home. Some of the lads have been getting pretty crook and it's little wonder. The conditions are appalling and disease spreads like wildfire.

I'm really worried about Stampy. Since leaving New Zealand he's got pretty scrawny. I've lost some condition too but not as much as Stampy — and there was less of him to start with.

Thankfully my health has improved in the past few days so it can't have been anything too serious. Nothing a good night out with the lads couldn't fix, anyway. I'm pleased to report that I'm in much better spirits after a trip to London.

Nine of us got a few days leave and we travelled there last Tuesday night. We left Sling at 5pm and arrived in the capital at 7:30pm. London is in bad shape these days with the effects of war everywhere. We still managed to have a good time though and a couple of days sightseeing was just what the doctor ordered.

Our first night was spent at the YMCA, which cost sixpence for a night's accommodation. Here we got a meal of sausage, egg, potato and a slice of bread for one shilling and threepence. Then we hung around to watch the changing of the guard. I'd have to say, Tom, despite all the marching and saluting, Buckingham Palace was quite impressive. I hope you get to see it one day.

After dinner we visited the famous Westminster Abbey and met up with two Aussie brothers called Derek and Curly Shaw. They turned out to be cousins of one of the lads in our section and by the end of the night we were all getting on like a house on fire.

I didn't play up too much though because we had to be up and away early next morning. There was a cross-country race at the Epsom racecourse and we were invited to participate. It was a great opportunity and I wanted to do well.

Our race was three miles round the track. It was another team event and I finished first in our group. There were some good runners there and we came second overall, so everyone was pretty chuffed.

After the race we got the train back to London and had a guided tour through St Paul's Cathedral. Blimey! Talk about good building skills. I've never seen the likes. The original building was erected in 604. Then it was rebuilt in 1675 after the Great Fire of London. They actually celebrated Queen Victoria's Jubilee here in 1897! Can you imagine? I've read about these things in history class but never thought I'd get to see them for real. The best part is the dome. A builder's nightmare at just over 121 yards high! But definitely worth a look.

The next day we boarded a train to Inverness with some of the Scotties we palled up with. The journey took most of the day and it was evening when we arrived. Great chance to take it easy. I love the Scottish accent and could listen to their yarns for hours. They sound just like the Jamiesons round in Felix Street.

One of the Scotties had family to visit and they asked us to join them. Everyone here is very friendly to those of us in uniform and we enjoyed our first taste of home cooking in months. The family was very hospitable and made us all welcome.

I really like Scotland, Tom. It felt familiar. It's smaller and less populated than England. More like back home, I suppose.

I was going to look up Dad's family but it turned out we were quite a way from Aberdeen so I decided to wait until next time as I'm sure there will be other opportunities.

We did manage to visit a fair dinkum castle though, complete with turret and drawbridge. This one even had a moat to stop enemy invasions. If there was anything we didn't know, the lads were more than happy to fill us in, and it was good to see some local history while we're here. Beats learning about it in a classroom any day.

Best regards,

Jack

North East Valley, Dunedin

Dear Jack,

Buckingham Palace! Jeepers! And a castle to boot. You really are seeing the world, eh. And living the high life too by the sounds of it. Ma said she wants to hear all the details when you get back. Every last one! She hopes you've remembered to pack your sketchbook.

Hopefully you'll get to Aberdeen next time. It would be nice to catch up with Aunty Doris and Uncle Hugh. Ma said Uncle Hugh works as caretaker at the local school so he shouldn't be too hard to find.

Love from
Tom

Sling Camp — Salisbury Plains, England

Dear Tom,

Things have started to heat up.

    This is a quick note to say that no one is getting any leave now. We have been told we are preparing to leave England soon so I'm afraid Aberdeen will have to wait a while.

    Will write again when I have more news.

    Best regards,

    Jack

North East Valley, Dunedin

Dear Jack,

I have been learning all about France at school. Mrs Stains showed us where it is on the map — directly across the sea from England and right next door to Belgium, Germany, Switzerland, Italy and Spain.

France's flag is red, white and blue — just like ours but they have a different design. Last time there was a war, they weren't on our side but now they are. And guess what they eat — frogs' legs! And snails! I wonder if you'll get to try some.

Do you know how to speak French yet?

I know that 'bonjour' means 'hello'. Mrs Stains showed me how to pronounce it. She also showed me how to say 'pass the jam please' but that might not be very useful.

Hey, Jack. I was wondering . . . If you have any leftover coins could you save some for me? That'd be great because I might be starting a coin collection soon.

Lots of love,
From Tom

Bonjour Monsieur Tom,

After ten hours by train and ship we have finally arrived in France. It's hard to believe we are actually here. I'm not quite sure what to make of the place yet. The camp we are staying at covers a large area and seems to be well organised. Morale among the troops feels mixed.

Apparently, the English papers are still reporting of great advances and the officers assure us the Germans are coming to the end of the road. We'll have to take their word for it, but I have my doubts that the Hun will roll over like everyone says they will.

By all accounts, the German forces are strong. Many say they seem just as well trained and equipped as us. Apparently their trenches are well dug and they've got sturdy pill boxes too, which are big, stocky concrete hideouts scattered everywhere to give them top notch protection.

One thing's for sure — the next few months won't be easy.

Two days later:

Things are moving fast. We have now been put into huts and briefed on what to expect for the next few days. Tomorrow there will be a twenty kilometre march with full pack, which means not much tucker to look forward to and even less sleep than usual.

We are going to be sleeping in dugouts and the commanding officer has told us a little about what to expect. Now that I have some idea about dugout conditions, I'm not looking forward to spending time in one. I've heard that soldiers often have to sleep on their feet.

And they say if you happen to look up at the wrong time you just might get your head blown off. Joves, Tom. This feels like very serious soldiering.

Wish me luck, mate. I think I'm going to need it.

Best regards,

Jack

Somewhere in France

Dear Tom,

We have been on the move for several days now, shifting camp daily as we make our way towards the frontline trenches. I hate to say it, but those Trentham route marches seem like a doddle compared to this. What was I complaining about, eh?

Good food is scarce as hens' teeth here. Rations are hard to come by and we eat what we find along the way. I'm not sure what we had for dinner last night or how long it'd been dead. Still, if I know what's good for me, I'll try not to give the matter any more thought.

Last night we camped in an old cellar near a ruined village. It was cold as heck but we managed somehow to stay dry. And in the morning we were lucky enough to come across a small supply of potatoes and turnips.

We are staying near a Belgian town called Ypres. The lads pronounce it 'wipers'. Like much of France this town's in a pretty bad way. Many of the villages are in ruins and it must be hard for the locals to carry on living here in the midst of such destruction.

Life would have been very different before the war. Apparently they grew delicious tomatoes and even made their own wine. I've heard there are still a few bottles in the cellars but no one has the stomach for it just now. With their old way of life in tatters, the villagers can't have much to look forward to. Beats me how they manage to keep going.

But the miracle is they do. And it's amazing how charitable and kind they remain. These people give the troops passing through everything they can. Their generosity is humbling.

Yesterday an elderly woman greeted us with a pot of soup. She'd been walking for miles and looked like she was at death's door herself. The soup was stone cold but offered with such kindness, I'd have to say it was the best thing I've tasted since leaving home.

Love from
Jack

France

Dear Tom,

This weather is a curse and we are up to our ankles in mud constantly. Last night I spent hours trying to scrape layers of the wretched stuff off my jacket and today I am sick to death of everything. I haven't washed in days and my body itches with lice. I am a revolting specimen and know I must reek to high heaven.

I shouldn't moan though. Apparently this is nothing compared to the Middle East. They reckon the lice and rats are nowhere near as bad as heat and dust and flies. Not by a long shot.

Four days later:

Feeling in better spirits today, Tom.

The weather has started to warm up and it makes a nice change to feel the sun on your face. It's also heartening to see a few violets and daisies poking through the ground. It'll be July before we know it and in the Northern Hemisphere that means summer.

I tell myself — if the flowers can muster the energy to hold up their heads in these frightful conditions, then so can I.

The vegetation is quite different here. The flowers are sweet and delicate. Lilies grow wild along the road, and yesterday we even found a crop of wild strawberries. They looked so tempting that we had to stop and I would have given my right arm for a bowl of cream and one of Ma's silver pudding spoons. It would have been heaven to sit on a dry blanket and feast on berries.

I've been feeling so homesick lately. I hope I've mentioned how grateful I am for your correspondence, Tom. Your writing helps to keep me sane. We all share our letters and it's such a comfort to know that life back home continues.

Some of the lads have sweethearts and some have children too. One bloke in our division, Charlie Walker, had word last week that his wife has given birth to a little girl. It breaks his heart to be so far away and he's desperate for news.

You can see why letters from home are so precious.

Mr Kidd writes now and then as well. I am quite worried about him. He says his son is still suffering from injuries he got at the Somme and I pray he manages to pull through. We all have to be grateful for small mercies.

Stampy and I play a game sometimes. It's called 'What I would give my right arm for'. It helps to pass the time and reminds us there is life apart from this wretched war.

You'd be surprised how cheap right arms come these days. Most of us would happily swap one for a warm bath, a pint of beer, some clean socks or even a night spent in clean bed sheets.

I think I would give both arms to see New Zealand again. To smell our Ma's corned beef hotpot, or hear Mr Gilbertson whistle, or see those great knobbly knees of yours all scratched and muddy from climbing the plum tree.

Best regards,

Jack

North East Valley, Dunedin

Dear Jack,

We all miss you so much. Mr Gilbertson is saving his best mutton savs for your return. He's got a stockpile in the safe and he says if you don't get back soon there'll be hell to pay.

I don't know if I could play that game of yours, Jack. I'm not sure I could give up my right arm for anything. How would I get to the top of the plum tree without it, eh? It might get Mrs Stains off my back though. I reckon she'd have to feel sorry for me if I had only one arm.

Maybe I'd feel different if it was me fighting in the war. I can't imagine what it must be like with the rain and lice and everything. It doesn't sound like much fun, that's all I can say. I thought it was supposed to be a lark. That's what you said before you left. Maybe you should have been a conchie instead.

Speaking of right arms, I couldn't knit without one, either. Knitting takes full concentration and very nimble fingers. That's what Mrs J says.

Take care, our Jack.

Lots of love,

Tom

Dear Tom,

Two nights ago I was in a reserve trench. Stampy was with me and it was the closest either of us have been to the Front. Just about did our heads in though. The noise was horrendous with shells blasting constantly and machine guns thundering like cannons overhead. It was the worst I've experienced yet and after a couple of hours I was shaking like a leaf. I still haven't recovered. Can't light a cigarette to save myself and my teeth rattle like bullets in my gums.

Sometimes I wonder if my nerves can stand it.

Later:

Miraculously, Stampy and I made it through the night. The next morning we were ordered to move forward to the trench we stand in now, which is scarily close to enemy fire. The trench is shallow, narrow and filled with the most disgusting sludge. It also stinks to highest heaven.

Next day:

We survived another night with just a few snatched minutes of sleep. They weren't kidding about the conditions in these trenches, Tom. My

God, it's bad. 'Atrocious' doesn't begin to cover it. It's a nightmarish hell and uncomfortable to boot. I don't think I will ever master the skill of standing up to sleep and the smell is beyond belief. The mud here is soaked in blood and the place crawls with rats.

I will write again later.

Best regards,

Jack

PS — Have just received some bad news. Poor Crofty got carted away with a shoulder wound yesterday and four others from our company are reported missing.

Please don't show this letter to Ma as I don't want her worrying any more than she needs. I know you'll use your own good judgement, Tom.

Dear Tom,

The last two days have been hell, with the enemy barrage as constant and deadly as ever. The Germans continue to pull no punches and many from our battalion are now on the casualty list, including my old friend Colin Marsh who copped a bullet to the side of the head. Mercifully, things have been quieter in the last twelve hours.

Regards,

Jack

PS — Yesterday Charlie Walker received a lock of his baby daughter's hair in the post and he is now the proudest man in Flanders.

Dearest Tom,

This afternoon we got ready with shovels and picks. Our orders were to repair the parapet of the trench. We knew it would be dangerous work and we were careful to keep our heads down. We were warned, under no circumstances, to look up. (Yesterday arvo two from the 1st Otago Battalion were bowled over and they don't want it happening again.)

Stampy and I kept our heads low and got on with the job as best we could. But within minutes, Fritz decided to make things interesting and sent across the most fearsome barrage, roaring across the sky like a thunderbolt. After that, we couldn't hear ourselves think and there was nothing to do but crouch low and wait it out. For two hours we held the shovels over our heads and tried to hold still. For the last half hour Stampy recited poetry while I did nothing but count the lace holes on my boots.

How we are still in one piece, I have no idea. But we are! And hallelujah for that.

Unfortunately, the same can't be said for the parapet.

Three days later:

I have just returned from wiring duty and very grateful to be still in the land of the living. It was touch and go for a while and I reckon I owe my survival to good luck more than good management.

We left the trench not long after midnight in a drizzly fog. It was the first time Stampy and I had been on wiring duty and neither of us knew what we were in for. Before we left we smeared our faces with burnt cork and removed all forms of identification from our pockets. (That's in case you get taken by the enemy.) We were both fully armed with rifles and grenades. Unfortunately for us, the fog was so thick that we only had a scant idea where we were headed. Even the flares didn't help much.

Talk about scared, Tom. It took every ounce of determination, daring and brazen good luck to make it under that wire and out across no-man's-land. And twice as much to make it back. We crawled on our bellies through the mud for more than three hours and I don't think I'll ever forget the stench in my nostrils or the icy fear that coursed through my body during that crawl.

Much love,
Jack

Dear Tom,

More bad news from the front.

I've heard that three more soldiers from the First Otagos didn't make it back last night. That's three more lads whose bodies will be left to rot in stinking Flanders sludge. I know it doesn't bear thinking about but today I can't think of anything else. Poor Charlie Walker. Do you remember me telling you about him? He was the one with the new baby. Anyway, poor Charlie was carted away on a stretcher in a pretty bad way. We don't know yet if he was alive or dead.

Surely things can't get any worse. My feelings change with each passing day. Last time I wrote I felt that luck was on my side — that someone upstairs was looking out for me. But today I don't feel like that at all. The sad truth is, we all live in fear of being shot. We're like animals being hunted. No more, no less.

You try not to let the situation get the better of you. And everyone gets through it as best they can. Sometimes I think it would be a blessed relief to suffer the worst and be done with it. But mostly I hang on for grim life, trying to make it through the next minute, or the next hour — or maybe if I'm lucky, the next day.

When I woke this morning I had such a heavy feeling in my stomach. Dread? Fear? Anger? Who knows? I lay there trying to work it out — how I felt about all that's going on. But nothing made any sense and the only conclusion I came to was we're all poor wretched souls who live each day a gunshot from oblivion. And that's the sorry truth of it.

One thing's for sure, Tom. I will be mighty pleased when this tour of duty is over.

Love from
Tom

The Western Front

Dear Tom,

I am writing this letter from a frontline trench. As I struggle to put my thoughts on paper I realise how grateful I am to the clever sod who invented the pencil. Who would think a simple piece of lead could help me give you, my brother, an idea about what's going on here? It's a miracle, Tom. You must agree.

Unlike this wretched farce of a war, which is the absolute opposite of a miracle. Ha! I guess mankind is responsible for good things as well as bad, eh.

Our enemy is not too far away today and the whiz-bangs have been going off steadily all night. You wouldn't believe the racket they make. There's a lull at the moment but who knows how long it'll last.

Trench warfare is difficult to describe. There are waves of near calm, and then chaos as the fighting flares up and dies back down again.

You have to be ready for anything.

It's a bit like being in the jungle with a tiger. You have no idea when your stalker is going to pounce and all you can do is hope you have the good luck to survive another night.

I suppose at the end of the day, it's all about luck, and I reckon if your number's up there's nothing you can do about it. Just like those rabbits you and Uncle Ced hunt. They don't have much choice either, eh.

Some of us make it and some of us don't. It's as simple and random as a game of cards. And these trenches are full of those who drew a bad hand.

Dear Tom,

It's been quiet for a couple of days now. Some of the lads like to play cards when it's quiet and others like to do bugger all. Some of us read or write letters. It's amazing what people read out here. The Bible is popular but one chap had a book by Jane Austen. She's an English writer and, so far as I can tell, her books are all about young ladies who swanned about in dresses a hundred years ago and fell in love with chaps who rode horses. There are plenty of horses over here, Tom. But we're a tad short on ladies in dresses.

One of the lads was reading the book out loud. It wasn't something I'd have cared for back home but I swear, when I closed my eyes, I almost forgot where I was for a while.

Chaps act differently in the trenches, Tom. They tell you things they wouldn't dream of telling you if you were back home. And you find yourself telling them things as well.

The weird thing is, we're all the same underneath. We might come from different places. We might be builders or work in the post office. We might be teachers or butchers or farm workers. But underneath it all, we're just the same. Scared to death with a serious job to do.

And we've all got different responsibilities. Privates, officers, field ambulance workers, stretcher carriers.

The stretcher carriers have the worst job, I reckon. Honestly! Those brave beggars put their lives on the line constantly, carting away the wounded. There was this bloke a couple of days ago. Things had gone quiet and we struck up a conversation. He confided that he was a conscientious objector from Timaru. A religious man who didn't believe in war, with a wife and child waiting for him at home. (A little boy just turned three.) So I told him about you and Amy and Ma and he shook my hand and wished me luck before trudging off in the mud.

Since then, I can't get the picture of him out of my mind and I haven't stopped thinking about him.

Dear Tom,

A few more quiet days at the front and thank the lord for that. This morning I wrote a letter to my old boss, Mr Kidd. Sadly, his youngest son, Bert, has died from the wounds he got several months ago. Bert wasn't much older than me and the apple of his father's eye so I can only imagine the sorrow they'll be going through.

I have to keep this letter short, Tom. Apart from the news about Bert I wanted to let you know that we are on the move again. I can't say much more than that but will let you know what's happening as soon as I'm able.

Take care, Tom.

Much love,

Jack

Belgium

7th June 1917 — Messines Ridge [*a strategic ridge near the town of Messines (Mesen) in Belgium. New Zealand and Australian divisions lie to the south-east*]

Bloody hell, Tom!

You'll never believe what's just happened. It's the most incredible thing and if I didn't see it with my own eyes I'd never have believed it.

We were in a trench watching the Messines Ridge. At 2:50am, there was an artillery barrage. The barrage had been constant for a while but it was nothing out of the ordinary. Then suddenly, everything changed. At around three o'clock, things heated up with an almighty explosion that blasted across the sky. The force of it was extraordinary. Joves, Tom. I've never seen the likes.

It felt like the end of the world and I truly thought we were all done for.

The earth shook violently and great flames of fire shot hundreds of feet in the air. An eruption of earth, rocks, flames and smoke spewed into the sky. It was like the bonfires of hell. One very massive explosion — I'd say about 300 feet high at least.

A split second later came a deafening roar. And the ground beneath us shook like the devil. The hillside cracked and thundered like Satan himself and it seemed like the world might be blown to smithereens. Smoke billowed out . . . then everything disappeared under a thick black haze. God Almighty!

It turns out a series of underground mines had been laid by the British, which must have taken some organising.

Soon after the explosion our orders came through. With gas masks on, we left the trenches en masse and made our way towards the chaos. Our whole division advanced across no-man's-land towards the hollow craters left by the explosions. We made our way from shell hole to shell hole, crouching down as low as we could. And my heart was fair pumping with adrenalin.

Our next orders were to move forward and take up position in the enemy trenches, clearing out all opposition as we went. But there was practically no need because the explosion had knocked the wind out of everyone's sails.

And the German troops were well and truly annihilated.

I'm not sure how many were killed in total but, for once, Old Fritz offered no resistance at all. In fact, those who survived just staggered towards us with hands in the air. They were disoriented and unsteady on their feet and most of them seemed only too relieved to be taken prisoner.

Poor beggars.

CROWN OF A YEAR'S WORK

CAPTURE OF MESSINES RIDGE

GREATEST SPECTACLE OF THE WAR

NEW ZEALANDERS' SPLENDID WORK

(AUSTRALIAN-NEW ZEALAND CABLE ASSOCIATION.)

LONDON, 8th June.

Mr. Philip Gibbs writes : "The Australians [!] and New Zealanders captured Messines in an hour and forty minutes, in the face of a desperate German defence, killing many of the enemy. The Irishmen captured Wytschaete, while the English took Battle Wood, south of Zillebeke. The Germans are now massing troops towards Warneton for a counter-attack. The Ypres salient has been wiped out.

"The Battle of Messines, which began at dawn to-day, was more audacious than the Battle of Vimy and Arras, because of the vast strength of the enemy's positions, and the massed gunfire was of greater intensity than in any of the previous battles. Our troops are now fighting forward through the smoke and the mist, English, New Zealanders, and Irish Protestants and Catholics, fighting shoulder to shoulder, made good progress up the slopes to Wytschaete and Messines. Prisoners are already telling how the British swept over and beyond the German positions, and the day goes well.

"Messines ridge for two and a-half years has been the curse of our men who were holding the Ypres salient. The Germans here had stacked up guns and every kind of explosive against us. The battle only started after the most complete preparations known to military science. A year ago miners commenced the tunnels for laying down the tremendous explosive 'ammonal,' which at a touch to-day blew up the hillsides, altering the very geographical face of France. Sir Herbert Plumer had been preparing for this attack for a year, and was ready a week ago with guns, 'tanks,' and every kind of explosive which modern science had designed for killing men in great masses. The terrible bombardment commenced a week ago, and increased in violence, working up to a supreme fury as the dawn broke. For five days the Germans had been pinned to their tunnels, and had no way of getting out of these zones of death. Regiments which attempted to come up last night were shattered by our heavy guns, which laid down belts of shell-fire, devastating and impenetrable.

"Our gunners also smothered the German batteries whenever the airmen revealed them. Our aviators have been wonderful. They have brought down forty-four of the enemy's machines in five days. Flocks of aeroplanes went up this morning, in order to blind the enemy and report on the progress of the battle.

"The men knew they were going to attack a Gibraltar, and expected that the enemy would fight his hardest for the Messines ridge. The final outburst of the guns was a most terribly beautiful thing, the most diabolical splendour yet seen in the war. Out of the dark ridges of Messines and Wytschaete and the ill-famed Hill 60 there gushed an enormous volume of flame from the exploding mines. A New Zealand boy who came back wounded said he felt like being in an open boat in a rough sea. The ground rocked up and down. Thousands of Anzacs [New Zealanders] and British soldiers were thus rocked before they scrambled up and dashed forward to the German lines, assisted by a tornado of shells, which crashed over the enemy's ground. White, red, and green distress rockets rose from the German lines, telling the gunners that the British were upon them. Soon these distress signals appeared no more— instead, were the British signals.

"The German prisoners began to come back in batches. They described the eagerness of the attackers as so great that they sometimes seemed to be in advance of the barrage. The Germans, who did not expect the attack for another two days, made a desperate effort at night to relieve their exhausted troops, but the new divisions lost heavily in coming up to the firing line. The story of this great victory cannot yet be told, but the reports show that our men everywhere succeeded in gaining their objectives with astonishing rapidity. Sir Douglas Haig's plan of battle was carried out on the field almost to the letter and the time-table.

"Irish Nationalists and Ulstermen, vying with each other in courage and self-sacrifice, stormed their way up to Wytschaete, and, after a desperate resistance, captured all that was left of the famous White Chateau. By midday our men were well down the further slopes of the ridge, while the field batteries were rushed up the ridge and took their new positions. The English, further north along the shoulder of the Ypres salient, captured the greater part of Battle Wood, south of Zillebeke."

North East Valley, Dunedin

Dear Jack,

Jeepers! The newspapers here are reporting a great victory. They said those Germans didn't stand a chance. They said they didn't know what hit them. Eighty thousand Allies were sent over the top. New Zealanders and tanks included. That's what the paper said. Just imagine . . . Nineteen mines exploding in just fifteen minutes.

What an effort. What a day!

We're going to win the war now, I reckon. Mr Gilbertson reckons so too. Even Mrs Stains says so. You'll be home before we know it. Nothing surer. You'll be home before we can say 'Jack Robinson'.

Lots of love,

From Tom

Back in France — July

Dear Tom,

I'm not sure if we're going to win this war or not.
I wish I were as certain as the men who write the
newspapers. Or you. Or Mr Gilbertson. Nothing
seems very certain here at all.

But someone must be looking after me because
I am now in France again. And I'm determined to
make the most of it.

We had a big night out last Saturday. I won't go
into all the details but there were a lot of hijinks and
some of the lads finished up a tad the worse for wear.

We are all living on our nerves these days, with
some poor beggars teetering over the edge. Dust
ups happen frequently and, after a few drinks, a
soldier can get out of control.

On Saturday one of our lads got mouthy with
some English bloke and he finished up with a
crack on the jaw and a black eye for his trouble. It
would have been okay but the situation escalated
when Billy and the lads stepped in to help.

As you might imagine, our Colonel wasn't
impressed. And, after some miserable sod reported
back to him, we all got a thorough dressing down.
He told us, in no uncertain terms, that we were a
disgrace to our units. Then, as punishment, he made
us do a three-hour drill march wearing our gas
masks. All I can say is, it's hard to believe we had

laid down our lives for our country not 24 hours before, eh.

Best regards,

Jack

PS — I saw my reflection in a mirror the other day, Tom, and I hardly recognised the bloke looking back at me. I'm thin as a rake with a whiskery beard and a crop of boils around my chin. Still, I can promise I'm not ready for the knacker's yard yet. Not by a long shot.

Dear Tom,

This army is certainly a hard place to fathom at times. The orders come straight from the top and those at the bottom have no choice but to do as we're told. I don't think the blokes in charge have much idea a lot of the time. It seems to be one rule for them and another rule for us.

Unfortunately, the more I know about those who give the orders the less respect I have.

Messines may be hailed a success but there have been some nasty cock ups with good men being sent into battle without proper thought of the risk.

Soldiers are dying in their thousands, for barely any ground at all.

Best regards,

Jack

Dear Jack,

I bet you don't have as many pimples as I have. I've got pus balls on my chin bigger than nail heads. I try not to look in any mirrors and I suggest you do the same.

We were reading your letter on Friday night when Mrs J came over. She reckons you sound just like our Dad. She said this war is making you old before your time. She said you were just a kid when you left and now you sound like an old man, whiskery beard and all.

I can't believe it's over ten months since you left. Ma said in some ways it seems like forever and in other ways it's hardly any time at all.

I played draughts with Amy again last night. She's getting crafty now and nearly won two games in a row. Guess I can't go so easy on her any more, eh.

We went to the pictures after that. Frank Morrison came too. We saw Buster Keaton and Charlie Chaplin. It gave us all a laugh.

Guess what? There's a dance in the church hall this Saturday. YWCA. But Ma said I'm too young to go yet.

Maybe next year, eh.

Love from

Tom

Dear Tom,

Sorry about my last letter, mate. I really should hold back on the details. I forget who I'm writing to sometimes and I'm sorry if I start to ramble. The sights you see here make you soft in the head and writing things down helps.

I should be grateful I can still hold a pencil. Some poor sods come back from the frontline unable to write their own names. Hell, some of them can't even *remember* their own names.

Shell shock is ghastly. One of our guys had it bad. He didn't say a word for days. Just sat in the mess tent staring at nothing. It was like his mind had gone AWOL on him. I think losing your mind must be a darn sight worse even than losing your leg. And it's no wonder some of the lads want to get the hell out of here. There's many a poor sod who's been shot for desertion.

Leonard Watson from our section found himself in a bit of strife the other day. We'd been under fire all week. Old Fritz was in a bad frame of mind and we were copping it big time. It must have been too much for poor Leonard because suddenly he just up and legged it.

Twelve hours later he was found wandering round no-man's-land without a clue who he was or even what division he was with. Poor bloke couldn't remember a thing. Luckily one of his mates recognised him and got him back behind the lines. Lord knows what would have happened otherwise.

The firing squad would have made mincemeat of him if they'd mistaken him for a deserter.

Best regards,

Jack

Hallelujah, Tom.

Today was a rare and joyous day. A fine thing to behold. Managed to forget about fighting for a whole night when we were treated to a performance by a New Zealand concert party. They call themselves 'The Tuis' and they travel around, performing for the troops. What a night we had, eh. Those lads fair lifted our spirits with a razzle-dazzle theatre performance. And after one stirring haka there wasn't a dry eye in the house. Today I'm feeling more homesick than ever but even more determined to make it back home.

Best regards,

Your brother, Jack

PS — Please thank Ma for the shortbread and the socks. They went down a treat.

PPS — Also thank Mrs J for her Baxter's remedy, which will definitely come in handy.

A poem by Arnold Wilson

(known to his friends as 'Stampy')

The Generals Calling the Shots

These trenches stink of filth and fear.
It's the generals calling the shots.
Of sludge and vermin and death so near.
It's the generals calling the shots!

Of demons and death.
Of a noose round your neck.
It's the generals calling the shots.
Of death and decay,
we're all in a bad way.
It's the generals calling the shots!

Let's run for the hills,
we should have made wills.
It's the generals calling the shots.
That's what they will say,
if the Hun get their way.
It's the generals calling the shots!

Go stand your ground.
The artillery's bound.
It's the generals calling the shots.
To fall a bit short.
That's when you'll get caught.
It's the generals calling the shots!

We should all be back home.
But to here we did roam.
It's the generals calling the shots.
To lend them a hand.
Now wasn't that grand.
It's the generals calling the shots!

What would they care?
If we all disappear.
It's the generals calling the shots.
That day might be near.
Bet they won't shed a tear.
It's the generals calling the shots!

There's death and decay.
Can't live through the day.
It's the generals calling the shots.
The night's even worse.
We're all under a curse.
It's the generals calling the shots!

They'll do you no harm.
But my mate's lost his arm!
It's the generals calling the shots.
We'll all burn in hell.
And we won't live to tell.
It's the generals calling the shots!

Hold it right there,
'cause your day might be near.
It's the generals calling the shots.
I've about had enough.
Can't you give me some snuff.
It's the generals calling the shots!

You'll get back on the horse.
We don't deal in remorse.
We're the generals calling the shots . . .

Dear Tom,

Last week Arthur Weir copped a bullet in his arm and got himself a 'Blighty'. The lucky beggar's off to England now for a spell in hospital. Seems everyone wants a Blighty these days and I reckon I wouldn't say no to a rest myself.

It's not that we're lazy, Tom. The kiwi soldiers are some of the hardest workers out. The ANZACs have a fine reputation and our divisions are well respected. We work hard behind the lines and our record is top notch. They say we've achieved all objectives so far and we helped win the battle of Messines. Some of the others haven't done so well and I've heard the French forces are in total disarray with soldiers even refusing to move.

Best regards,
Your brother, Jack

Dear Jack,

The school hols are nearly over and I spent most of them chopping firewood and doing chores for Ma. Not that I minded too much, 'cause at least I managed to go hunting with Uncle Ced for a couple of days. I took our Jacky on some nice walks as well. He's going fine on his leash by the way.

To be honest, not having to go to school was such a treat that I didn't much care what I did.

Mrs J came to visit last night and we had a singsong round the piano. I don't know how many times they sang 'It's a Long Way to Tipperary' but it must have been at least a hundred. Then they both got tipsy on sherry. Ma got all tearful from singing and Mrs J made it even worse by reading out Stampy's poem. Then they both got on their high horses and started on about the Prime Minister and the war office. Mrs J was ranting and raving about conscription and Ma was agreeing with everything she said for once.

Mrs J reckons the kiwi soldiers have done their duty three times over. She reckons enough's enough and if she had anything to do with it you'd all be on a troop-ship home. She's going to write a letter to the Prime Minister about it next week. Ma says she'll write one too. Fat chance.

I wish you could get a Blighty back to New Zealand, Jack. I'm sure they could carry the war on just as good without you. What difference would one soldier make, eh? Maybe I could write to the Prime Minister myself. If I told him about our Dad dying and Ma staring out

the window all the time they might let you come home.
Surely there's special leave you're entitled to.

I can't wait for you to come home.

Take care of yourself, Jack.

Lots of love,

Tom

PS — Don't forget about the zoo, will you. Our Amy is worried that you won't remember. She's drawn you a picture of a giraffe so you don't forget.

Somewhere in France

Dear Tom,

The frontline is getting closer all the time.

We've been on the move for almost a week, marching most of the day. It's a long, slow trudge and our packs weigh a bleeding ton.

Last night we bivvied down in an old barn, and tried to get what sleep we could. This morning our orders were to move up to a new position opposite some German machine guns. Can't say I'm not shitting bricks here now, Tom, 'cause I am.

It's pretty hard not to when you're this close to enemy lines.

Close to the Western Front

Dear Tom,

The German trenches are now only 600 yards away. It was so quiet on patrol last night that we could hear their soldiers talking. It was the first time I'd heard Old Fritz up close before and, even though I don't speak German, I reckon I had the gist of his conversation. It might sound strange but I don't think our enemy sounds too much different to us. And the voices I heard could well have been Bill and Stampy, if I didn't know better.

It's an odd thing to say, I know, but I reckon those soldiers sounded just as sick of this war as we are. Their voices sounded as weary and fed up as us. And just as scared as well.

It got me thinking, Tom. We're all the same underneath. Our blood is the same colour — there's enough evidence of that here. But there's more to it than that. We've all got lives and loved ones back home. And I reckon this war's gone on for long enough!!

The other day Stampy found a photograph — from a German corpse's pocket. The chap in the photo was in his bathers at the beach. This chap could have been anyone, Tom. Like me or Bill or Stampy. Or you, Tom. (Well, maybe not Stampy 'cause I can't imagine him in bathers.) And the beach could have been St Clair beach. Or Brighton. It looked just like our beaches back home. And it made me wonder why I should want these men dead.

But war is a funny old thing because an hour later Old Fritz had shelled us yet again. With an accurate dose of shell fire he'd managed to kill three of our men and blast Malcolm Blaney's lower arm off.

Might suspend my sympathies for just a bit longer, eh.

Two days later:

Another day, another exchange of fire. Getting more used to trench warfare these days.

There were shells bursting all around and the noise was ear-splitting. But then the weather turned sour.

The Germans always get the upper hand when the weather goes bad. Fritz chooses the ground with care and his positions are higher and drier than ours. Unfortunately, the British trenches are not as well constructed and more likely to fill with water and sludge.

This time, after a very strong barrage our Sarge called the order to advance and off we went, clambering up the hill. Old Fritz had waited until we'd left the trenches before opening fire. Then he let us have it. We hadn't got far before things turned to custard.

We struggled for a while, shin deep in sludge and unable to see too far ahead. The conditions were atrocious now. Hail fell in sheets and men dropped like flies. The place became a bloodbath in minutes and the sensible thing would have been to retreat except that the officers continued to order the attack. So we had no choice but to do as we were told.

Finally, an hour and a half later we were ordered to dig in where we were. It was too late for those who had copped it already but the rest of us took our chances and tried to dig back in, under heavy fire. Luck was on my side this time and I found shelter in a shell hole. I'm not sure exactly what happened next. There was a lot of confusion and my brain was all fuddled from shellfire. I think I must have been knocked out though because next thing I knew I was on a stretcher being carried behind the lines.

A doctor informed me I'd lost a lot of blood and I could feel pain on the side of my face. I was lucky to get some first aid before losing any more blood.

Feeling mighty relieved, as you can imagine.

Will write again when I'm feeling up to it.

Take care back home.

Your loving brother,

Jack

July

Dear Tom,

I'm feeling better now and the other lads have filled me in on some of the details about what happened. My face must have swelled up pretty bad after that because I was sent straight to the first aid post. There were two other chaps alongside me and what a state we were in with me bleeding like a stuck pig and the other two not looking much better. Between us we had missing teeth and a broken arm, and one poor sod had half his leg blown off. The doctors did what they could but it was obvious that we all needed more attention and were sent on to the casualty clearing station.

We left the clearing station about ten that same night and were taken by motor ambulance to the hospital. We arrived around four the next morning. It was a rough ride but I was relieved to be finally out of there. Things had become pretty serious for the bloke with the wounded leg though and I'm not sure about the third chap because, by this time, I was having trouble with my sight. My eyes were swollen shut and my mouth was split and bleeding. I felt like I'd just gone five rounds in the boxing ring.

I stayed in the ward for three days before being transferred. I didn't see the bloke with the leg injury again so I assumed he'd been taken straight away.

Counting my lucky stars I'm still alive.

Love from

Jack

August

Dear Tom,

Looks like I finally got my Blighty and can't say
I'm disappointed. My wound must have been worse
than I thought because I have now been ordered
back to England. I was hoping to meet up with a
couple of the lads from my section but I haven't
seen anyone yet. I haven't heard from Bill either,
but I did get a letter from Stampy.

Dear old Stampy — he has become such a good
friend over these past few months. I don't know how
I would have got this far without him. He's a damn
good mate and someone you can trust your life to.

(And to think I once doubted his abilities as a
soldier.)

Back in England

Dear Tom,

We sailed to Dover and waited in the train for
the next lot of wounded to be shipped in. They
were coming thick and fast that day — boatloads
of broken lads, with head injuries, missing limbs
and bullets lodged in all sorts of unmentionable
places. It just goes to show what sort of bloodbath
this war has become.

I'm in hospital now, and looking at some of the wounds here I know I've been lucky. Some of the lads are paying a high price and I have to be grateful for having most body parts intact. At least I've still got four limbs. And I haven't had to give up my right arm either. Not yet, Tom.

The worst thing I face these days is not being able to eat much. With the old jaw being out of action there'll be no mutton chops on the menu for a while.

My orders are to follow a light diet of easily swallowed food. Custard goes down not too badly and the nurses bring me bread soaked in milk every now and then. It's not the tastiest food in the world but better than Machonochie's or bully beef. And it's a relief to be out of bombing range for a while too, I reckon.

Best regards,
Jack

North East Valley, Dunedin

Dear Jack,

Jeepers! You really have been in the wars lately. (Pardon
the pun, as Mrs Stains would say.) I guess the best thing
you can do is try and enjoy your Blighty.

Mrs J sends her love and says there's a letter coming.
So does Mrs Stains and Mr Gilbertson. Everyone wishes
you a speedy recovery but Ma says 'not too speedy'. Mrs J
has just discovered some new pills that help you put on
weight and she will put some in her next parcel. She said
to tell you to be on the lookout.

We're thinking about you all the time, Jack. Amy was
actually calling out to you the other day. She can get quite a
way up the plum tree now. She's got sturdy legs and a head
for heights. Not like me who gets all giddy in the tummy.
Anyway, Uncle Ced made us a ladder and Amy was under
strict instructions not to go any further than the fourth
branch from the top.

What an imagination that girl's got.

Amy reckons she can see Europe from up there, Tom.
She reckons England's just over the hill.

'Let's talk to our Jack,' she said to me the other day.

'But he's in England, Amy,' I said.

'I know. But England's just over there,' she said,
straight as a die.

'Over where?'

'Over that hill,' she said, pointing to Pine Hill. 'Mary

Brownley told me. And she said if you shout really loud they can hear you.'

So that's what we did (hollered like hillbillies) and I hope you could hear us, Jack, because we yelled so loud we almost lost our voices.

Lots of love,

From Tom

North East Valley, Dunedin

Dear Jack,

We haven't heard from you in a while. Where are you now? Are you still in England? Or are you back at the frontline?

I know my letters are getting shorter but it's hard knowing what to say these days. Telling you about my stamp collection seems silly now. And writing about knitting seems even sillier. Mrs J is hovering around as usual. And Ma still spends a lot of time in her room. Nothing is very exciting here in North East Valley and we're all missing you heaps.

I'd be grateful for another man about the place, that's for sure. When is this war ever going to end, eh?

Please come home soon, Jack.

Lots of love,

From Tom

England

September

Dear Tom,

Joves, mate. Sorry I haven't written in a while. But don't let that stop you sending your chatty cheerful letters. They buck me up no end and make life more bearable than you'll ever know. I look forward to the sketches and the scribbles too. Not to mention the scarves and honey and socks. And, of course, Mrs J's latest remedies are always welcome.

Please tell Ma I've had the operation and the doctors say there should be little disfigurement, which is a good job if I'm going to impress the young ladies. Also, I'm hoping for just a hint of a battle scar, which could make me look mysterious and interesting.

The stitches have been taken out from the inside of my lip and the outside ones will stay in for a bit longer. The doctor says I've been lucky not to lose my teeth. Unlike the poor beggar in the next bed who got a piece of shrapnel in the top corner of his mouth and lost his whole top set.

Take care and give my love to everyone.

Best regards,

Jack

North East Valley, Dunedin

Dear Jack,

Ma says to stay in hospital for as long as you can. She says to keep your head down and don't be in a hurry to get back to France. Bide your time, Jack. That's Ma's advice. I think she's hoping this war will be over before you get out of hospital. That's what the papers are saying these days.

And Mr Gilbertson agrees.

Mrs J says she'll believe it when she sees it and why hasn't the Prime Minister replied to her letter yet.

Hey Jack. Guess what?

Frank Morrison's sister is going to be a nurse. She's doing her training and wants to go to England soon. Ma is getting all morose. (That's a new word for melancholy I learned from Mrs Stains.) Ma says what's the world coming to when all our young lads get shot overseas and our young ladies have to go and help stitch them back together again.

Love from

Tom

September

Dear Tom,

Frank's sister is in good company, I think. The nurses here are total angels and very pretty as well. There's one in particular I've taken quite a shine to. Her name is Jennifer Skelton and she comes from a place called Bath.

You'd like her, Tom. She tells me she has a dog called Rosie. A corgi of all things. Her people are from Scotland and she has a sister about the same age as you. We seem to have struck up quite a friendship. She's been nursing for just a few months. I told her we call Dunedin 'The Edinburgh of the South' and she likes to hear what it's like.

I've told her all about the North East Valley and our school and the fun we have in Lindsay Creek. And you and Ma and Amy. And Mr Kidd. I've told her about Mrs J too. And our Dad. I've told her about my plans to be a carpenter too. She said she wants to come and visit us. Who knows, she might make it over when this war is done and dusted. Fingers crossed, eh.

The ward I'm in is mostly full of head patients. A right sight we must look too — all wrapped up like Egyptian mummies. The nurses read to the lads with eye injuries and I've started reading the paper to an English soldier called Gordon.

Poor Gordon had a bad dose of gas and doesn't

know when his sight will return. I've also been reading him *Tom Sawyer* because one of the soldiers had a copy. Have you read it, Tom? It's by an American writer called Mark Twain and it's a great yarn. I'm only a few chapters into it but it's all about this young boy called Tom. At the start of the book he plays hooky from school and has to whitewash the fence for his Aunt Polly. But he has such good powers of persuasion that he ends up getting everyone else to do it for him. Tom's best friend is Huckleberry Finn (I love that name). Huck Finn doesn't go to school often on account of his father being the town drunk. I was put in mind of you and your friend Frank Morrison — not that Frank's father is the town drunk but I know the two of you are tip-top friends.

Yesterday Gordon confided to me that he is engaged to a young lady in Wales. Obviously he is anxious to regain his sight. But will his young lady still want him if he returns home blind? That's the worrying thing.

He's in a terrible state about it. I tell him it won't matter. If she loved you before, she'll love you again, I say. But in my heart I'm not so sure. Poor sod. I'd hate to be in his shoes.

On the bright side, we are all treated very well here. Some of the patients even get the odd trip to London and parcels arrive from the Red Cross on a regular basis. It's a treat to see what's inside. The last one contained a copy of the *Otago Daily*

Times. It was amusing to read the 'entertainment' section but not so amusing to read the 'roll of honour'. It really brings it home when you see the names in a printed list like that.

Money-wise Blighty is not so good. We can only draw sixpence a day wages when we're in hospital, which doesn't go far at all. Still, compared to the other chaps in here I have nothing to complain about. And, after looking at the latest 'roll of honour' I realise I have a mighty lot to be thankful for.

Best regards,

Jack

North East Valley, Dunedin

Dear Jack,

I looked up Bath in the atlas yesterday. It took me ages to find because it's such a small word. I only found it in the end because Ma thought it was near a place called Bristol.

Oh, and guess what? Mrs J had *Tom Sawyer* in her bookcase and she is letting me borrow it. I've read the first chapter already and, you're right, it's a great story and gallops along at a good pace. I really like the part about the whitewashing. Thanks for recommending it.

Lots of love,
From Tom

Hornchurch, England

Dear Tom,

I have been discharged from hospital now. They've given me fourteen days leave before I have to go back to Sling and then to France. I am staying in a village called Hornchurch, fourteen miles out of London.

I guess I'm in two minds about going back. Part of me wants to make the most of my Blighty but the other part knows the lads need all the help they can get at the Front. And I wouldn't feel right not pulling my weight.

Besides, I think something important may be coming up. A big push, by the sounds of it. If that's the case then they're going to need all hands on deck to make it work. One thing's for certain — we have to get it right this time because the ANZACs can't go on losing good men. Not like they have these past few months.

Fingers crossed, Tom. I may be home for Christmas after all. Let's hope so.

Missing you all like crazy.

Lots of love,

Jack

NEW ZEALANDERS IN GREAT FORM

CONQUEST OF THE HIGHEST POINT

(Received October 6, 11 a.m.)

LONDON, 5th October.

Mr. Gilmour, correspondent for the Australasian Press Association, writes that he saw the New Zealanders going up to the front. They were greatly relieved that they had not been overlooked. Their greatest anxiety has been lest the "show" should be over before they were given their chance. They were in great form, having been resting since Messines; and they were never keener to meet the enemy. The New Zealanders closely co-operated with the Australians, in the same difficult sort of terrain as their previous assaults.

The Anzacs were chosen for the push slightly north of the front they had occupied at the commencement of the offensive, and had to advance across slightly rising ground, and secure the ridge north of Polygon Wood, which was the highest point necessary to obtain complete command of the whole of the Passchendaele Ridge. Otherwise the British line would be subject to a constant menace.

Sir Douglas Haig, by this third rapid assault on the same wide front, has wrenched from the enemy the whole of the high ground. It has been proved that nothing the enemy can do is able to stem our advance behind our terrible artillery barrage. The Germans' only hope lies in counter-attacks, in which they inevitably suffer heavily under our bombardment. The Anzacs will be delighted at finding themselves in a position to look down on the ground where the storm of shells is bursting over every vestige of the German defence.

BRITISH ATTACK RENEWED

HAIG REPORTS GOOD PROGRESS

ON A WIDE FRONT AT YPRES

The New Zealand High Commissioner reports :—

LONDON, 4th October, 11 a.m.

Sir Douglas Haig reports : East of Ypres, at 6 o'clock this morning, we again attacked on a wide front.

Satisfactory progress is reported, and a number of Germans have already been taken prisoner.

(AUSTRALIAN-NEW ZEALAND CABLE ASSOCIATION.)

(Received October 5, 8 a.m.)

NEW YORK, 4th October.

The British are winning all along the line.

THE YPRES ATTACK

ADVANCE A MILE DEEP

Dear Jack,

Yahoo, big brother! What a battle! What a victory!

The *Otago Daily Times* was full of it. The attack at Broodseinde on 4th October has been hailed as a great success for the Allied forces. The headmaster read the news story out loud to everyone in assembly.

He said that two Otago battalions were involved along with battalions from both Auckland and Wellington. When he said that, there was an almighty cheer. The whole hall erupted. Then he read out another bit that said 'ANZACs fought like tigers'. And everyone cheered again.

The paper said the Allied attack at Broodseinde was 'Germany's biggest ever defeat'.

'Four ANZAC divisions attacked side by side, advancing up slopes armed with strong points.' And the Germans were taken completely by surprise. The headmaster said the New Zealanders performed well and took all their objectives. He said when the British artillery erupted at dawn hundreds of Germans were slaughtered by the fire and the soldiers moved up the hillside with little enemy opposition. The best news is, the ANZACs have advanced the line by 1900 yards. We all went out to the rugby field and stepped the distance out, just to see how far it was. It's a fair way, Jack. But not as far as you'd think.

Anyway, the headmaster said it means the Allied powers can finally win the war.

Yay, for that!

Love from Tom

Back in France again

Dear Tom,

It seems like everyone has been spurred on by the ANZAC attack on 4th October. Despite all the casualties they say it was an important strategic victory. I guess I'll take their word for it. Nothing feels too much like victory here at the coalface, but that's another story.

Luckily our good reputation continues and the next step is to capture the nearby village. Let's hope the Germans are in for another drubbing, that's all I can say.

Two days later — quick note to family

Awaiting orders, camped out somewhere in France

The weather has got worse since I last wrote. And the lads are concerned about the speed this attack has been put together. It all seems a bit rushed from our end but then we have to put our faith in those who are in charge. And we need to trust that they have some idea about what they're doing.

Fingers crossed, young Tom.
Much love to you all,
Jack.

North East Valley, Dunedin

Dear Jack,

We are all so proud of you here in North East Valley.
    And we can't wait for Christmas.
    Take care.
    Love from
    Tom

Belgium

October 11, 1917

Dear Tom,

Still here. Still in one piece. Can't ask for more than that.

Tonight we are making preparations for a major offensive. We arrived at this camp a few days ago. What can I say? It's close to the trenches, near a small village in Belgium. This village is our ultimate target.

Our orders are to lie low until 3pm and then move forward in artillery formation. It's been decided. The second Otagos will go over the top in the first wave. I'm glad to be going first. Get it over with, eh.

It beats waiting around. And if all goes well we should have captured those German trenches by midday. So long as the barrage is strong and the wire gets cut they say she'll be ours for the taking. Let's hope so.

By the time you get this letter it should all be done and dusted. Mission accomplished.

Keep your fingers crossed, young Tom. And maybe your toes as well.

Best regards,
Jack

I'm drifting in and out of sleep.
Memories crash through my
head like surf on sand. A tui
sings in a place far away. A
place called home . . . perhaps.
The spiky fronds of cabbage
trees block my view. Silence
deafens me.

At the edge of sleep an elephant
hovers.

There is nothing to do now,
but wait. Dread sits stale in
my stomach like a lump of old
coal. My mouth is parched with
fear and my heart aches with
longing.

I am more scared today than I
have ever been in my life.

North East Valley, Dunedin

Dear Jack,

Last night I had a dream. I was at the Wellington Zoo. Everyone was there. You, me, Ma and Amy. Even Mrs J. And Uncle Cedric. Mr Kidd came too. He'd taken a week off work. I was allowed to ride the elephant first. I sat way up high above the whole world while everyone clapped and cheered from down below. We had ice cream for afters — with strawberries on top.

But this morning, the telegram man came down our road on his bike. As soon as I saw him I knew what it was. So I closed my eyes tight and said the Lord's Prayer. Twice!

I never say the Lords' Prayer normally, not even when we're supposed to at school. But I did today. 'Our father ... Who art in heaven ... Hallowed be thy name ... Thy kingdom come ... Thy will be done ...'

I said it as hard as I could.

But all the time I was thinking about elephants, Jack. And you. I could see you with my own two eyes. Large as life and twice as handsome, as our Dad used to say.

But when the telegram man slowed down I knew the Lord's Prayer wouldn't be enough.

So I tried to make myself stop breathing because I thought, if I could only make myself go still, no one would have to die. Ever again. Ever, ever again. I held my breath until my heart was pounding in my ears. Like the sea.

I could hear Ma in the wash house. Humming. She'd been happier lately. And she hadn't stared out the window

in days. Please God, I thought. Make him go away. Please
... Please ... Please ...

But the telegram man wouldn't go away. He walked
straight up to our door and knocked hard. Bang. Bang.
Bang.

'Is your Dad home?' he said in a croaky voice. I could
see his Adam's apple wobbling in his throat.

'No,' I said.

'What about your Ma?' he said.

I shook my head. I plugged my fingers in my ears.

I can't remember what happened next.

But somewhere in the house someone started to cry.

British Army Field Hospital

October, 1917

Dear Mrs McAllister,

It is my sad duty to inform you that your son, Private Jack Donald William McAllister, was killed in action at the Battle of Bellevue Spur on 12th October, 1917.

The assault on the German positions occurred four miles east of Ypres and just west of the village of Passchendaele in Belgium. The 2nd Otago Battalion suffered grievous losses that morning and experienced desperate fighting, under the most intense machine-gun fire. Your son fought gallantly till the end and has fallen nobly. He has fought proudly for the King and Empire.

Please accept my sincere condolences and deep personal sympathy. I hope you obtain some comfort in the knowledge that your son has responded bravely to the Call of Humanity, Freedom and Civilisation.

Yours very sincerely,

G. M. Bathgate

Brigadier General

Second NZ Brigade.

Humanity . . . Freedom . . . Civilisation . . .
Mrs J tossed her head back in disgust when she read that.

'Is that what they're calling it these days,' she said. And when our Jacky tried to snuggle on her knee she pushed him straight off.

Mrs J came over a lot that week. 'Just to keep an eye on you all,' she said.

Everyone cried and cried and cried. This time I cried even more than Ma. I cried about everything. I cried because our Dad was dead. And now my brother was dead as well. I cried because the war was still going and no one was ever going to surrender. I cried because the whole world was fighting and now I wouldn't get to ride an elephant.

But mostly I cried because, without our Jack, life would never be the same again.

I cried for two whole weeks without stopping. I heaved and sobbed until I nearly couldn't breathe. No one could make me stop. Not even Mrs J.

A few weeks later another letter arrived. It had a bright green stamp on it — a special wartime edition starring King George the Fifth.

Dear Mrs McAllister,

My name is Arnold Wilson and I was good cobbers with your son Jack.

I am writing to let you know exactly what happened on October 12. I would like to give a true account because that is what you deserve. It's what everyone deserves.

The facts of the attack are as follows:

October 11. The rain hadn't stopped in more than a week. The place was a bog hole and the troops were in no fit state to fight. The barrage started at 5:25pm. At zero hour our orders were to crawl out to no-man's-land. Jack and I were going 'over the top' first. We hadn't had a wink of sleep and felt scared to death, both of us. Something wasn't right and everyone knew it. For the first time we made out our wills before going into battle. There was a whole battalion in the first wave and we had ten minutes to get to no-man's-land. This was an unreasonable request, even in good conditions. But in the army you do what you're told. Our orders were to rush the first trench, kill or take prisoner everyone in it and then, after fifteen minutes, withdraw back to our line.

That was the plan.

We waited nervously, our stomachs tied in knots. Everyone smoked cigarettes, even those who didn't smoke. When the guns lifted the sergeant called the order. Advance!

Jack was with me but slightly ahead. With mud up to our shins we advanced as best we could up the hill. It was a long, slow slog. Jack was a fit man, as you know. Long-legged and strong. He forged on ahead. I followed close behind. But it was a struggle and I could feel myself floundering. I lost my boot at one point and had to stop. By this stage most of us were firing randomly. It was chaos.

Men dropped like flies, while their mates forged on ahead. Some just yelled their heads off. It was madness.

Most men were shot in their tracks. Some were killed by friendly fire. And those who made it to the wire didn't stand a chance. They were in for a shock. The wire wasn't cut and all our men were hung out to dry.

They died in droves, that day. Like lambs to the slaughter, we didn't stand a chance in hell. The whole Otago battalion was almost wiped out. Only 32 of us survived — 148 out of 180 were killed.

I am sorry if this letter disturbs you, Mrs McAllister. But I wanted to tell you the truth. Your Jack was a good mate and if the boot was on the other foot I know he'd do the same.

Your Jack always did his best. He went the extra mile. I'd like to tell you he died with no pain. But you don't deserve to be lied to. Your Jack died doing his duty. Whether those generals did their duty by him is a different matter.

Your family should be proud of Jack. He was a great soldier and a great mate. He was a bloke with a big heart and a head on his shoulders. He loved his family and talked about you often. He was serious about his work and would have made a fine carpenter. I am honoured to have known him.

Best regards,

Arnold Wilson (Stampy)

Jack McAllister was a private in the 2nd Otago Battalion. He joined up when he was 18 and he was 19 when he died.

He died at Passchendaele, along with many thousands of others. (Six per cent of New Zealand's total casualties in the First World War occurred in just one morning of action on 12 October 1917.)

By all accounts Jack and his mates didn't stand a chance. The Germans knew they were coming and had a grand old time wiping them out. Nothing went right that day. Our artillery might as well not have been there. The mud was thick and deep and our artillery couldn't move forward. Those who did get within range had no solid foundation from which to fire. The ground slipped below them. The New Zealand soldiers were picked off by enemy snipers quicker than you could say 'Jack Robinson'.

It was a bad time for New Zealand. Around 17,000 New Zealanders were killed in the First World War and another 41,000 were wounded. New Zealand's population at that time was just over one million. Lots of boys were just like our Jack. They went away to war and never came back.

Many of them lie buried at Tyne Cot cemetery in Belgium.

The First World War ended just over a year later — on 11 November 1918 — when the Armistice (peace treaty) was signed.

I guess you're wondering what happened to the rest of us. To Ma and Amy and me. And Uncle Ced and Mrs J. Well, we cried a lot at the start. I was angry as heck. So was Ma.

We wanted things to get back to normal but that would take a lot of time. Jack's friend Stampy came to see us. He brought us letters and what was left of our Jack's sketchbook. He brought Jack's possessions home, which helped — a bit.

We all went to Wellington in the end. We even had a ride on an elephant. It was Mrs Jenkins who made us go. One day she came over and Ma was lying in bed, staring at nothing and wondering what our world was coming to. And Mrs J said, 'Come on, Jess.' Then she flung back the curtains and said it was time for the grieving to stop.

Of course, Ma wasn't having a bar of it. She said, 'What are you on about, Nola? This grieving will never stop.'

And Mrs J rolled her eyes and sighed. Then she made Ma a cup of tea and sat on the edge of her bed. She held our Ma's hand.

'Do you want all this to be for nothing?' she said.

'Do I want all what to be for nothing?' said Ma.

'Your Jack's death,' said Mrs J.

'I don't know what you're on about,' said Ma.

Then Mrs J took a sip of tea. 'Why do you think your Jack gave his life in the war?' she said.

Our Ma shrugged. 'No one knows the answer to that,' she said. 'It was a bad idea from the start.'

'Of course it was,' Mrs J said. 'But it's done with now and there's no changing it.'

Ma shrugged and pushed her tea away.

Mrs J was having none of it.

'Go and get your glad rags on, Jess,' she said.

Mrs J folded her arms and waited. Ma didn't have the energy to argue.

'We're off to Wellington on the 24th of June,' said Mrs J. 'I've made the booking and I'm not taking "no" for an answer.'

Ma knew there was no point in arguing. Maybe she even knew that what Mrs J was saying was right.

'You owe it to your Jack,' said Mrs J. 'We all do. If your Jack gave his life in the war then it's our job to make it worth his while.'

So that's what we did.

fter the war they made a monument. It stood right in front of our school.

Lest we forget, it said.

'What does that mean?' Amy asked.

'It means we must never forget,' said Mrs J.

'Forget what?' said Amy.

'We must never forget what happened, when our Jack went to war.'

WAIST DEEP IN MUD

—

FOLLOWING THE BARRAGE

—

ADVANCE UPON A FORBIDDING STRONGHOLD

—

(AUSTRALIAN-NEW ZEALAND CABLE ASSOCIATION.)

LONDON, 18th October.

Bellevue Spur is an ugly V-shaped hill, rising to a height of 200 feet above the flooded Rabapeek Creek, its sides extending 1000 yards back into Passchendaele township. At the point of the V, which is about 200 yards wide, a deep concrete structure stands overlooking our lines, with narrow slits, manned by machine-gunners and snipers, governing every approach. Two irregular lines of wire, each ten feet deep, extend across the front of the reboubt down the hill to the valley, where a smaller redoubt bars the flank. Bellevue looks a forbidding stronghold, and was the scene of one of the greatest incidents of the war.

Against this spur thousands of fine-spirited New Zealanders flung themselves at dawn on Friday, with high hopes of crowning an unbroken series of victories with the greatest victory of all. The enemy barrage played heavily upon them for twenty minutes before the start, but the lads rose eagerly from a line of shell-holes and began a steady advance wave, our barrage plunging ahead. The men sank sometimes waste deep in mud. The barrage went faster than advance was possible. The enemy machine-gun fire swelled to a shriek, and many men fell, but the others pressed on. They reached the Rabapeek and plunged into this deep morass. The enemy's main barrage of shrapnel and high explosive descended hereabouts, whilst machine guns, which were now thickly studded in the trenches between the redoubts, seemed to close the passage over the stone road which traverses the morass. Many, nevertheless, pressed irresistibly over the dead and across the road, others plunging through the water, though wounded, and some were drowned.

THE EFFORT FADES AWAY

Then the ascent of the slope began, and the first wave, which was now thin, reached the wire. This heroic effort will in future be told wherever Australasians gather. The gallant lads tried every means of piercing the wire. Wave after wave advanced to death. Many were riddled with bullets, and the others dropped to the ground and began crawling beneath the wire. Many who were shot remained where they fell. Some reached the other side, charged, and fell. One reached the redoubt and began to crawl beneath the slits and round to the side. Perhaps he might have altered the fortunes of the engagement with bombs, but he was killed by one of our rifle grenades, which we were firing from shell-holes. The great effort ended. The waves had determinedly expended themselves. The survivors remained in shell-holes, the Jaegers sniping so accurately that any head put above the ground was shot. They awaited another effort, which the commanders decided was undesirable. The line was organised at night-time, but later was somewhat withdrawn, in order to permit the shelling of the enemy position.

The day was crowded with heroic incidents. An orderly-room sergeant, after the death of the colonel and the wounding of the adjutant, went through a hail of bullets to the senior captain, found him wounded, and went to other senior officers, who were all disabled. He went to a lieutenant, and informed him that he was in command of the battalion. The journey occupied ninety minutes. A Lewis gunner, who was wounded, the rest of the crew having been killed, continued to work the gun upon an enemy machine-gun, twice advancing the position alone, and finding another gun when his own was blown out.

Our Jack's Will

In the event of my death I bequeath all money in my paybook to my mother — Jessica Mary McAllister.

I bequeath all my sketches to my sister, Amy.

And I bequeath my carpenter's nail bag to my brother, Thomas Andrew McAllister, in the hope that he puts it to good use.

THE
END

GERMANS ACCEPT DEFEAT

ARMISTICE SIGNED YESTERDAY

WORLD--WIDE REJOICING

Wellington, Nov. 12.

(Extraordinary)

THE ARMISTICE WITH GERMANY HAS BEEN SIGNED.

(Signed) W. F. Massey.

WHAT DO YOU KNOW ABOUT THE FIRST WORLD WAR?

WHAT WAS IT?

The First World War was a military conflict that began in 1914 and ended in 1918. It involved nearly all the world's major powers. Partly for that reason, but also because of the very high death toll, it has been called the Great War and 'the war to end all wars'.

HOW DID IT START?

War broke out when Austria declared war on Serbia after a Serbian terrorist assassinated Archduke Ferdinand of Austria on 28 June 1914.

For years beforehand, countries in Europe had been forming alliances and building military arms and forces. This had led tensions to build up to the point where the assassination provided the trigger for war.

There was a general sense of excitement in 1914 when war first broke out. Armies were quickly formed. Young men longed for adventure and everyone expected the conflict to be over in a matter of weeks.

WHO WAS INVOLVED?

The opposing alliances were the Allied Powers and the Central Powers.

- The Allied Powers included: Russia, France, the British Empire, Italy, the United States, Japan, Romania, Serbia, Belgium, Greece, Portugal and Montenegro.
- The Central Powers included: Germany, Austria-Hungary, Turkey and Bulgaria.

There was great rivalry between Britain and Germany. Britain was the first country to make steamships and railway engines. But Germany was fast catching up.

HOW WAS WAR WAGED?

In the old days armies used to move from place to place and there were planned battles with clear winners and losers. This war would be different, partly because of the new weapons of mass killing that were now available.

This time Germany decided to capture Paris from the north. Then Britain joined France and they began a 'race to the sea' to try to gain control of the ports along the English Channel.

Within three months, both sides had dug trenches all the way from the Belgian coast, through northern France and almost to Switzerland. They stayed there for four years — gaining and losing ground in equal measure.

WHAT WAS TRENCH WARFARE LIKE?

The soldiers lived, ate and slept in trenches, which were overrun with rats and lice and the partly buried bodies of dead soldiers. The trenches were lined with sand bags and protected with barbed wire. No-man's-land was the area between the opposing trenches.

The Germans generally built trenches on higher ground. As a result they were deeper and safer. They also had more machine guns and were able to gun down British soldiers as they advanced up the slopes. The British and French trenches were shallower and more prone to flooding.

One of the reasons for the high loss of life in the First World War was that the army commanders were still planning old-style battles, relying on sheer force of numbers to rout the enemy. They were slow to adapt to fighting with machine guns, heavy artillery and poison gas.

HOW DID THE WAR END?

In March 1918 it seemed as though Germany had won. The German Army had broken through the British and French defences and it looked like the Allies were finished. But the German soldiers were exhausted and couldn't keep up their advance. So the British Army took advantage of the situation and advanced from France into Germany.

Germany surrendered on 11 November 1918, and an armistice was signed.

HOW MANY FOUGHT AND DIED?

- 65 million troops were mobilised.
- More than 9 million troops died on the battlefields, and 21 million were wounded.
- Many more millions died on home fronts because of genocide (organised mass murder), food shortages and ground combat.
- 11 per cent of France's entire population was killed or wounded.
- 58,000 British troops were killed on the first day of the Battle of the Somme, 1 July 1916.
- More than 200,000 men died in the trenches.
- The First World War saw the first known use of chemical weapons. These included mustard gas, chlorine, phosgene and tear gas. They were used to flush the enemy out of their trenches so that the guns could finish them off.
- The infantry still fought with traditional weapons: rifles and bayonets. But now they had to face flame-throwers, machine guns, heavy artillery and tanks, as well as gas.

WHY DID NEW ZEALAND AND AUSTRALIA GET INVOLVED?

As members of the British Empire the politicians felt duty bound to offer their resources to help defend Britain.

Initially men between 19 and 38 were accepted into the army. Some men joined 'to see the world', have some adventure, to escape unhappiness, see the mother country or defeat 'the barbaric Germans'. Others joined simply because their mates were going. Some needed a job; the army paid five shillings a day for New Zealanders and six shillings for Australians.

ANZAC (Australian and New Zealand Army Corps) forces were offered to the British Army to use however and wherever its commanders saw fit.

THE PRICE NEW ZEALAND PAID

In 1914–18, the New Zealand population numbered slightly more than one million people.

- 120,000 in total were enlisted or were conscripted.
- 103,000 served overseas.
- 550 nurses served with the NZEF.
- New Zealand suffered 58,000 casualties (17,000 killed; 41,000 wounded).

THE PRICE
AUSTRALIA PAID

At the time, Australia had a population of slightly less
than five million people.

- 416,809 in total enlisted or were conscripted.
- Australia suffered 216,000 casualties (60,000 killed;
  156,000 wounded).

New Zealand and Australia had among the highest
casualty and death rates per capita (per head of population) of anywhere in the world.

AUTHOR'S NOTE

I stumbled into World War One history quite by accident, as the idea for this book evolved from a very different project.

During my research I was touched by the letters and first-hand accounts of soldiers.

I began with just one basic fact: my great-uncle John had been killed at Passchendaele during World War One. Until five years ago I had never heard of Passchendaele and I had no idea what had happened there. But the more I read, the more absorbed in the details I became, and the more admiration I developed for the brave young men who went so naïvely off to war out of a sense of loyalty, duty and even adventure.

I began to wonder what it must have been like for those who waited back home. How did they cope with the uncertainty? How did they carry on with their lives in the face of such disruption? And how did they make sense of their losses as the appalling 'roll of honour' grew?

As a country of less than one million people, New Zealand paid a high price for the so-called 'Great War'.

I have no idea what my great uncle wanted to be when he grew up. I have no idea what sort of work he did before he left home. But I do know that he came from an intelligent working-class family and I'm sure he could have done much with his life if he'd been given the chance.

I liked the idea of 'Our Jack' having been a carpenter.

Apart from being an honest, hard-working occupation, there is something symbolic about those young lads leaving their 'nail bags' behind. And I like to think it's up to those of us lucky enough to have been born post-war to honour their memory by creating a country they would be proud of.

Some books that helped my research

Zero Hour: The Anzacs on the Western Front by Leon Davidson
    (Text: 2010)
Nice Day for a War: Adventures of a Kiwi Soldier in World War One
    by Chris Slane and Matt Elliott (HarperCollins: 2011)
Massacre at Passchendaele: The New Zealand Story by Glyn
    Harper (HarperCollins: 2000)
Dark Journey: Three Key New Zealand Battles of the Western Front
    by Glyn Harper (HarperCollins: 2007)
Letters from the Battlefield: NZ Soldiers Write Home, 1914–1918
    by Glyn Harper (HarperCollins: 2002)
The Diary of a Young Soldier in World War 1 by Dennis Hamley
    (Franklin Watts: 2001)

ACKNOWLEDGEMENTS

In writing this story I am deeply indebted to many historians and authors who have written about World War One before me. I am also grateful to have had access to some published family histories in the Dunedin Public Library.

I would like to acknowledge historian Glyn Harper, whose writing has made me aware of the tragedy and importance of Passchendaele. And to all those brave young men who wrote to their families so regularly and so well.

Special thanks also to our historical advisor, Ray Grover, who gave his time and expertise to ensure the details in this book were accurate.

And to the *Papers Past* website, produced by the National Library of New Zealand. Your resource is invaluable.

Finally, a big thank you to Barbara Larson whose hard work and loyalty is always much appreciated.